KC banged on the darkroom door.

"Peter!" she cried. "It's KC! Are you in there?"

The door opened, and Peter looked at her calmly. "What's up?" he asked.

"What's up???" KC shouted. "I thought you were killed or seriously injured!"

"Why would you think that?" Peter asked.

"Why do you think?" KC demanded. "You didn't show up at the party tonight. What other explanation could there be?"

"Some of us just have other priorities."

"Huh?" KC asked, dazed at Peter's flip attitude. "Did you forget we had a date?"

"I know you said something about a party," Peter said, "but I didn't think it was a big deal." He walked back into the darkroom. "Anyway, I had some important work I wanted to catch up on."

KC followed him inside. "Peter," she pleaded, almost in tears. "I don't understand. Why are you doing this to me?"

Don't miss these books
in the exciting FRESHMAN DORM
series

Freshman Dorm
Freshman Lies
Freshman Guys
Freshman Nights
Freshman Dreams
Freshman Games
Freshman Loves
Freshman Secrets
Freshman Schemes

And, coming soon . . .

Freshman Fling

FRESHMAN CHANGES

Linda A. Cooney

HarperPaperbacks
A Division of HarperCollins*Publishers*

Thanks to Carin Greenberg Baker

HarperPaperbacks *A Division of* HarperCollins*Publishers*
        10 East 53rd Street, New York, N.Y. 10022

Cover art by Tony Greco

First printing: June 1991

Printed in the United States of America

HarperPaperbacks and colophon are trademarks of
HarperCollins*Publishers*

10 9 8 7 6 5 4 3 2 1

One

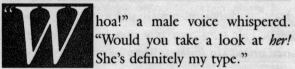

"**W**hoa!" a male voice whispered. "Would you take a look at *her!* She's definitely my type."

"Keep dreaming," another guy said. "She's the Freshman Princess. She wouldn't look at you cross-eyed."

KC Angeletti was within hearing distance, standing by the salad bar in the University of Springfield Dorm dining commons. She was used to getting this reaction. Even before being crowned Freshman Princess at the annual Winter Formal, KC had always turned heads. Ordinarily she didn't care, but today she took it as a happy omen. If two guys she didn't know thought she looked great, then Peter Dvorsky was bound to think so, too. Not that he ever seemed to notice *what* she looked like, but things were starting to heat up between them. Any minute now, he might come wandering through the door to the dining commons, and when he did, KC was planning to dazzle him—with restraint, of course. It wouldn't pay to look too eager.

Leaning toward the shiny, aluminum hood over the salad bar, KC examined her reflection. Her face was distorted from the curve of the metal, but she noted with satisfaction that her long, dark hair glistened and her gray eyes sparkled. Her trim navy blue suit hung crisply from her broad shoulders. *Watch out, Peter,* KC mentally warned him, *I'm going to* make *you notice me this morning.*

Not that there was too much competition at this hour. KC straightened up and scanned the dining room with its rows of dark, wood tables. Most of them were already filled with drowsy young men and women, their hair standing up in combed clumps. Though KC witnessed this frumpy spectacle every morning, she still couldn't understand how people could appear this way in public.

"Somebody point me in the direction of an empty table," Winnie Gottlieb mumbled sleepily as she shuffled toward KC with her breakfast tray. Her muddy running shoes squeaked against the linoleum floor and her black, silk kimono flapped open to reveal neon green running shorts and a man's tank undershirt. Her spiky, brown hair, which normally stood up straight, now flopped around her face like dozens of wilted antennae.

"Why don't you just open your eyes?" KC suggested as Winnie stopped beside her and rested her head on KC's shoulder.

"My eyes are on a timer," Winnie said. "They don't open before ten A.M. I can't believe I signed up for a Friday morning class. What could I have been thinking of?"

"Come on, Winnie," Faith Crowley laughed as she followed a few steps behind her friends. "It's seven-thirty. Hardly the crack of dawn." Faith's golden hair escaped in wisps from her French braid, and she wore an old, unraveling cardigan sweater and faded jeans.

"There," KC said, nodding her head in the direction of a long table with four empty seats at one end. "I think that's the best we're going to do." KC gently pushed Winnie's head to an upright position. Then she strode briskly toward a table beneath a large picture window framing distant mountaintops.

The three girls had become best friends in junior high school and were still an inseparable trio even though their first semester in college had pulled them in different directions. KC was the go-getter of the group. She wanted to be a business executive and thought getting ahead meant making the right social connections—such as joining a sorority. Winnie, on the other hand, thought sororities were for snobs. She wasn't about to change her wild and wacky ways. She was a free spirit, for better *and* worse. Faith was the one who kept the trio balanced. She was steady and thoughtful, and was already getting a reputation on campus as an up and coming director.

After the girls sat down, KC watched Winnie rip open a paper envelope of artificial sweetener and pour it on her sugar-frosted cereal.

KC cocked one eyebrow. "New diet?" she asked. "Not that you need one." Small and compact, Winnie was a compulsive exerciser with a tight, firm body.

"I know this looks weird," Winnie said, "but I'm trying to cut down on sugar."

"Not me," Faith said, spooning brown sugar onto her oatmeal.

Before digging into her watery, scrambled eggs, KC removed a compact from her purse and checked her face. Her eyes still sparkled and her skin was satiny smooth. Nonetheless, KC patted her face with powder.

"You look great," Winnie said. "Like you just stepped off the cover of *Vogue.*"

"Or *Business Woman Today,*" Faith added.

"Making the rest of us mere mortals look like the shlubs we really are," Winnie finished.

KC frowned. Was she making it too obvious that she wanted to look good for Peter? Knowing how much her friends liked to tease her about him, KC tried to get Faith and Winnie off the track. "Laugh all you want," she said. "I can take it. Besides, now that Tri Beta's finally invited me to pledge, I don't have any choice. A Tri Beta has to look good all the time, or she's letting her sisters down."

This wasn't a lie. Beta Beta Beta was one of the most exclusive sororities on campus, with the best-looking, most well-connected girls. Now that KC had finally gotten in, after months of frustrating setbacks, she was going to make sure she *stayed* in. Her whole future depended on it. Being in the sorority would give her valuable contacts when she graduated and entered the business world.

"I understand completely," Faith said, nodding. "It's just a sorority thing." She smiled as she sliced a banana into her hot oatmeal.

"Oh, but don't worry," KC said, leaning forward. "I'm not going to get so caught up in Tri Beta again that I'll forget who my real friends are. I promise I'll always be there for both of you, no matter what happens."

Winnie's brown eyes, peeping over the top of her orange juice glass, grew serious for a moment. She swallowed and put the glass down. "You know," she said, "I never thought I'd be able to get used to the idea of you as a sorority sister. I was afraid those mannequin girls with their goldplated fingernails had brainwashed you forever. I thought you'd forgotten about me and all the other people you knew from your previous life."

"The Tri Beta Stepford Sisters," Faith agreed.

Winnie laughed. "But now that we're friends again, I guess I can share you. Sorority girls aren't as bad as I thought. I even like Courtney Conner."

"I do, too," Faith said. "I used to think she was stuck-up just because she was president of Tri Beta, but I obviously had her all wrong. And she's been a good friend to you, which makes her okay with me."

KC smiled. "How does that old camp song go? *Make new friends, but keep the old . . ."*

"Yeah," Winnie giggled. "And isn't it funny

how new friends can be male as well as female?" Winnie and Faith exchanged an amused look.

KC froze for a moment. Then she composed her lips into a tight smile and said, "I don't know what you're talking about."

Faith laughed out loud. "You don't fool us for a minute, Kahia Cayanne Angeletti. You may be a Tri Beta, but we know the *real* reason you're looking and feeling so good this morning."

"And we know his name, too," Winnie said. "Peter Dvorsky."

KC blushed. "Is it that obvious?" she asked. "I guess you guys have known me too long."

"Since junior high school," Winnie said. "Which qualifies us as mind readers."

Faith leaned forward, elbows on the table, and rested her face in the palms of her hands. "Come on, out with it," Faith said. "How are things going with Peter?"

KC sighed and cut a piece of ham. "Slowly," she said, lifting a forkful of ham halfway to her mouth. "But I like it that way. I mean, if he'd come on too strong, I might have gotten scared away, but we're both taking our time. The more I get to know him, the more I see in him." KC's fork drifted back down toward her plate, the ham uneaten.

"That's better than jumping right into something with a guy you're infatuated with, then discovering he's not as great as you thought," Winnie said. "That used to happen to me all the time."

KC nodded. "I'm just glad Peter's stuck around after all I've put him through," she said.

Even though Peter had forgiven her, KC still felt awful when she remembered how she had invited him to the Winter Formal, only to dump him when someone better-looking came along. How could she have been so superficial? Peter wasn't gorgeous, but there was nothing wrong with the way he looked. And he certainly had a lot more on the ball than most of the spoiled, rich boys at the fraternities.

Peter was a talented photographer whose offbeat humor made KC look at herself honestly. That was painful sometimes, but KC always felt better for it. And the funny part was, the more time she spent with him, the cuter he seemed.

"Yoo hoo, KC!" Winnie called in a high voice. "Earth to KC! I think she's on Cloud 9," Winnie said to Faith.

"I'm sorry," KC said. "Did you say something?"

"Yes!" Winnie spooned the last soggy flakes from her bowl. "I wanted to know if Peter's kissed you yet!"

KC shook her head. "We haven't even been out on a formal date. I just danced with him at the party at his dorm, and we went hiking up at Hosmer Lake."

"But something will happen," Faith said emphatically. "I can feel it in the air. You *will* be kissed. Which is more than I can say for myself these days. I don't even know anybody I'd like to kiss, except my old teddy bear."

"Don't feel too sorry for yourself," Winnie said. "Just weeks ago you were kissed by one of the hottest movie stars in the country, or have you already forgotten about Alec Brady?"

"I'm not feeling sorry for myself," Faith said. "But I'll probably never see Alec again." Faith had apprenticed on the set of a Hollywood movie shot on campus, and she and Alec Brady had had a brief romance. "It's okay, though," Faith went on. "I'm going to be real busy soon, and I won't even have time to think about guys."

"A new drama project?" KC asked with interest.

Faith nodded. "I'm going to be directing a segment of this year's U. of S. Follies. It's sort of a slapped-together musical/variety show, but at least it's in the University Theater, so I'll get a lot of exposure. We're holding auditions next Wednesday."

"How about a high wire act starring me?" Winnie joked. "You could string a rope across the stage and I could walk across it, singing about how unstable my love life is. Only it wouldn't be an act, it would be real. *My story's sad to tell,*" Winnie began to sing in a mournful voice, pretending to balance herself with her hands. *"About a love that was going so well. Her name was Winnie, his name was Josh, but she screwed up, and oh my gosh."*

KC felt bad for laughing, since she knew how much Winnie had suffered since her break-up with Josh Gaffey, but she couldn't help it. "Not bad for off the top of your head."

"Winnie had two guys but couldn't choose," Winnie continued, changing the melody with every line, *"and so, dumb girl, both loves did lose."* Winnie hung her head sadly at the end while KC and Faith applauded.

"I guess it's good I can joke about it, right?" Winnie said, looking up. "I mean, maybe there's still hope for me and Josh. He did call when I was working at the Crisis Hot Line and tell me how much he loved me and that he was going crazy without me. Of course, he didn't know I was working there and that it was me on the other end of the line. So he doesn't know that I know, and I can't sit down and discuss it with him because he's really busy working on a big research paper. He's either coming or going to the Computer Center, and I don't feel like discussing our relationship when I'm running to keep up with him."

"He'll slow down eventually," Faith said, "or maybe you can figure out a way to shortstop him."

"Yeah." Winnie unwrapped a straw and stuck it in a glass of chocolate milk. "I could just leap out from behind a bush and throw myself on top of him. That's what I used to do to get a guy's attention." Winnie blew through the straw, making light brown bubbles on the top of her chocolate milk. Then she took a long sip.

"It's going to work out," Faith said with assurance. "When two people want to be together that badly, they find a way to make it happen. Look at Lauren and Dash. They had their problems, but now they're closer than ever."

"Where's Lauren been keeping herself?" KC asked casually. "I haven't seen her around."

Lauren Turnbell-Smythe was Faith's roommate. A creative writing major, Lauren also wrote for the campus newspaper, the *Weekly Journal*. Her ease with the written word made Lauren the person who could save KC's life. KC had been doing terribly in English all year. If she didn't bring up her grade, her average wouldn't meet Tri Beta's minimum requirement, which meant she could wave Tri Beta goodbye.

KC was determined not to let that happen. She'd signed up for another extra credit paper, but getting started was proving impossible. Maybe Lauren could help her.

"Do you need to speak to her about something?" Faith asked.

KC considered lying to cover up her problem, but then she relaxed. If she couldn't trust her two best friends, who could she trust? Faith and Winnie would understand.

KC sighed. "I was sort of hoping she could help me on my latest English comp assignment. We have to write a persuasive essay on any current topic, and I just can't seem to focus on anything. Since Lauren's so disciplined about her writing, I thought she could give me some pointers."

"I'll leave a note on her bed," Faith said. "But if you're in a hurry, why don't you get a tutor to help you?"

"A tutor?" KC asked. "Where can I get one?"

"At the Learning Center," Faith said. "It's like a resource room to help students with any academic problems they might have."

"Hmmm . . ." KC brightened. "Does it cost

much? I mean, I'm not as broke as usual. My grandmother sent me money to cover my sorority dues, but I only have about thirty dollars left."

"That should probably be enough," Faith said. "It's just one paper, so it shouldn't take more than one or two sessions."

"With me, who knows?" KC groaned. "If only all my courses were as easy as my Intro to Business course. That one's a natural for me. I mean, it's not as if I'm not trying in English, because I really am, but I'm having so much tr—" KC stopped in mid-sentence and the worried look on her face dropped away instantly.

KC had been so absorbed in her problems, she hadn't noticed Peter Dvorsky appear near her table. He was of average height and average build, with hair that was somewhere between blond and light brown. He wore a red baseball cap and a gray U. of S. sweatshirt. He was partially turned away from the table, as if he hadn't noticed KC sitting there, but he could easily have heard what she was saying. It was bad enough he wasn't impressed with her looks. KC didn't want him to think she was a crummy student, too.

"—I'm having so much trouble remembering the name of that movie I wanted to see," KC finished the sentence, smiling at her friends.

Winnie and Faith looked at each other in confusion. Then Peter suddenly turned around.

"Well, well, well!" Peter said, suppressing a smile. "Who do we have here?"

KC tried to keep her expression cool and distant, but she felt her face grow hot. "Hello, Peter," she said in what she hoped was a casual voice.

"Looks like all the tables are full," Peter said, looking around.

He wanted to sit with her! KC felt like bouncing in her seat, but instead she said, "There's an empty seat here, if you can't find anyplace else."

Peter shrugged. "Guess I'll have to take you up on it," he said, coming around the table and sitting down next to KC. "Very executive-looking suit," he joked as he pulled his chair closer to KC, so that their legs were nearly touching. KC felt goosebumps rise on her flesh. "I hope I didn't interrupt a breakfast meeting."

"Oh but you did," Winnie chimed in. "We are KC's high-powered business associates. I'm Winnie Spike, vice president of chocolate milk, and this is my colleague, Dr. Faith Broud, hot cereal specialist."

"Pleased to meet you," Peter laughed, though he was still looking at KC. KC, too, couldn't take her eyes off him. He looked as if he had just rolled out of bed, or off a baseball field, and KC knew she looked as pressed and clean as a Chairwoman of the Board. But despite their mismatched appearances, KC felt they fit together perfectly.

"I guess you've noticed KC's a little better dressed than we are," Faith said, "not that these aren't my best jeans. But did you ever stop to wonder why, of all the hundreds of freshmen breakfasting here this morning, she alone has taken the trouble to make herself look beautiful?"

"Ooh! Ooh! I know!" Winnie yelled, raising her hand in the air like she was waiting for a teacher to call on her.

"Yes, Winnie?" Faith asked, pointing with her spoon.

KC shot an alarmed look across the table. Faith and Winnie wouldn't really blow her cover, would they? After six years of friendship, they would allow KC just the smallest scrap of dignity, right?

"I think KC was hoping to run into someone," Winnie said. "A special someone. And I think she wanted to look good for him."

"And do we know the *name* of that special someone?" Faith asked Winnie.

KC shot her leg out to kick Winnie under the

table, but only succeeded in banging her toe on a metal rung of Winnie's chair.

"I don't remember," Winnie said, "but I think it rhymes with Meter. Let's see, could it be Liter? Heater? Jeeter?"

"You guys . . ." KC begged, her toe beginning to throb.

"Don't be embarrassed, KC," Peter said in an off-hand tone. "Even if you did go to all that trouble on my account, it wouldn't make any difference. I wouldn't care if you wore a mink dress and a diamond tiara."

"Well maybe *you* don't," Winnie jibed at Peter, "but your *eyes* certainly do, 'cause right now they're stuck on my good friend KC."

Two

Later that day, Lauren Turnbell-Smythe lay on her stomach on Dash Ramirez's black and white checked sofa, staring at her calculator. The numbers weren't adding up. No matter how many times she worked it out, the total was still less than zero. How could that be? After working long hours every weekend as a maid at the Springfield Inn, Lauren was facing something she had only read about: poverty.

"I like the way you crunch numbers," Dash flirted from where he sat on the bare wooden floor of his rented room, surrounded by dozens of sheets of crumpled paper. He was busy working on his latest article for the U. of S. Weekly

Journal. "I always took you for the creative type, but you haven't taken your eyes off that calculator. They must be giving you a lot of homework in your personal finances class."

Lauren rolled over onto her back and closed her eyes. "I wish it were for my class," she whispered, running her fingers nervously through her wispy, light brown hair. "A case study is easy to solve because all the answers are at the back of the textbook. But I don't think I'm going to be able to look up the answers to this one."

"What's the problem?" Dash asked, sliding over on the floor until his head was right above hers. "Maybe I can help."

Lauren opened her eyes and gazed lovingly up at her boyfriend. His dark hair was pulled back into a ponytail, and two days' growth of stubble shadowed his lean face. A red bandanna, which he usually wore on his head, was tied loosely around his neck. Just having him near made Lauren feel safe and secure, and almost made her forget her financial worries.

"Go ahead, pick my brain," Dash said. "I'm not a math major, but I did get a 670 on my SATs." Dash looked down at her tenderly, his face moving closer to hers.

"Kiss me first," Lauren said. "That will be my

spoonful of sugar to help the medicine go down."

"What medicine?" Dash asked, but Lauren shook her head and pointed to her lips. "Anything you say," Dash said, brushing her lips softly with his.

Lauren's blood began to fizz and a warm feeling spread from her lips down to her toes. The sensation was so pleasant that Lauren didn't want the kiss to end. But it was time to face reality. As Dash leaned away from her, Lauren sat up on the couch and grabbed a yellow legal pad. "Which do you want to hear first?" she asked. "The bad news, or the bad news?"

Dash sprang up onto the sofa, and put his arm around her. "I'm a man," he said, making his deep, Latino-accented voice sound even deeper. "I can take it."

"I'm poor," Lauren said. "In less than one year, you've seen me go from riches to rags."

"And I respect you for it," Dash said. "You stood up to your mother, you stood up for your principles, and now you're making it on your own, without any financial help from her." When Lauren had first arrived at U. of S., her wealthy parents had provided her with everything money could buy: a BMW sedan, a personal computer, CD, TV, and microwave oven. That all changed, however, when Lauren refused to join Tri Beta, her mother's sorority. Lauren's mother, furious at her daughter's rebellion, had cut her off without a cent.

"Standing up for my principles sounded good, in theory," Lauren said, "but I've just worked out the numbers, and somehow I come up several thousand dollars short by the end of the semester."

"No way!" Dash protested. "I thought you got a couple thousand when you sold your BMW."

"I did," Lauren said, "but it was banged up pretty good after Winnie had her accident in it. I didn't get very much. And it all went toward my tuition this semester."

"Well, what about your job?" Dash asked.

"That covers the rest of my tuition," Lauren said. "But there's nothing left for books or transportation or food, not that I really need to eat all those fattening meals in the cafeteria." Lauren stared ruefully at her slightly pudgy stomach, confined by the waistband of her black parachute pants. Pulling the sides of her antique, patchwork vest over her stomach, she buttoned it closed.

"You look good to me," Dash said, nuzzling her neck.

"I'm not going to look too good at the end of

the semester when I can't pay all my bills."
Lauren removed her round, wire-rimmed glasses
and placed them on the aqua blue, amoeba-
shaped table next to the sofa, a leftover from the
apartment's previous tenant. Then she hid her
face in Dash's hair. It smelled clean and fresh,
like lemons and soap.

"We'll think of something," Dash said, rising
from the sofa and pacing to the opposite end of
the small room in his high-topped sneakers. He
paused by the "kitchen," really just a row of appli-
ances against one wall—an old 1950s refrigerator
with rounded edges, a freestanding double sink,
an oven range from the 1970s, and a beige,
Formica counter.

"I could sell my soul," Lauren suggested wistfully.

Dash's dark eyes took on a demonic gleam and
he rubbed his hands together. "I happen to be in
the market for a good soul," he cackled. Then his
face relaxed again and he paced over to the
barred window overlooking a fire escape.

"I'll spend every free minute I have helping
you figure this out," he said. "We just have to
find a solution before Monday."

"That's right," Lauren said. "I forgot you've
got that special journalism seminar coming up."

"Every weeknight for the next two weeks,"

Dash said, staring out the window. "But we have a couple of days until then. Let's work on it right now. I'm sure we'll come up with plenty of good ideas. We're both intelligent, creative, incredibly talented people."

"Not to mention humble," Lauren said. She grabbed her glasses off the table and put them on. "Where's my pad?" she muttered, rummaging around on the sofa. "As we think, I'll write things down." She grabbed a pencil from underneath the sofa.

"Okay," Dash said. "First option. Generous relatives. I don't suppose your mother would relent and let you back into the family."

"Only if I joined Tri Beta, and that's never going to happen. Besides, I'm never going to ask her for anything ever again."

"We'll save that discussion for another time." Dash paced back across the room to the front door. "How about *my* parents?" Dash suggested. "They really like you, and they can spare the money. I'm sure they'd be happy to help."

Lauren didn't know whether to laugh or cry. Until a few weeks ago, she had assumed Dash was a streetwise kid from a poor family. It was certainly the impression he wanted everyone to have. So Lauren had tried to camouflage her upper crust background when she met the

Ramirezes, only to discover that Dash's father was the president of a bank and his MBA mother was chief administrator of a hospital. The funniest part was how entirely the situation had reversed itself—and for real. Now she was the poor one, and they were the ones with money. But even if she were starving, Lauren knew she could never ask Dash's parents to help her. "It's really nice of you to offer," Lauren said, "but I really can't accept. I won't take money from *anyone*. This is *my* problem, and *I'll* figure out a solution."

"*We'll* figure it out," Dash corrected her. He plopped down on the sofa and put his arm around her again.

"I could get another part-time job," Lauren said thoughtfully, chewing on the worn-down eraser on the end of her pencil. "Maybe the Springfield Inn would let me waitress on the days I'm not cleaning rooms."

Dash looked at her sternly. "When would you have time to write papers and study for exams? You're already taking one extra course this semester, not to mention all the work you're doing at the Journal. I'm surprised you haven't turned into a zombie already."

"I do feel like I'm walking around half-asleep a lot of the time," Lauren admitted.

"Maybe you should give something up instead of taking on more," Dash suggested.

"Don't even think it," Lauren said defensively. "I know what's going through your mind. You think I should stop working at the Journal because it takes up so much of my time."

"I never said . . ." Dash began, but Lauren cut him off.

"There's no way on earth I'd *ever* give up working for the newspaper," Lauren said. "It means more to me than any of my classes. I'd rather drop out of school altogether than drop the Weekly Journal."

"Well, something's got to give," Dash said, slumping back against the black and white checked sofa cushions. "If you can't increase your income, maybe you can cut expenses."

"How?" Lauren asked. "I'm only buying essentials, like books and toothpaste and stuff like that."

"I mean the big expenses like room and board. My rent is a lot less than what it costs to live in the dorm. And I spend half on food than what it costs you to buy a meal contract."

Lauren's violet eyes opened wide behind her glasses. "Are you suggesting that I move off campus?" she said in her soft, breathy voice. "But my room and board are already paid for. How will that save me money?"

"You can sell your dorm and meal contracts," Dash explained. "Then with the money you get, you can rent a cheap room. I know there are rooms in the area for even less than I'm paying."

"Move off campus . . ." Lauren said even more softly. She gazed from Dash's mismatched kitchen to the barred windows to the cinderblock table. How could she give up her cozy room, and her funky, creative dorm where the halls were constantly filled with singing, dancing, and paint fumes? And how could she leave Faith? Faith had been her first friend on campus, no, even more than that, the first friend who genuinely liked Lauren for herself, not for her parents' money and social connections.

"It's not so bad," Dash said, sensing her thoughts. "You might miss being around your friends all the time, but you'll still see them on campus."

Leaving Faith would definitely be the worst part. But there was something else Lauren had never considered, apart from saving money. Moving off campus would mean taking the final step toward independence. For the first time in her life, she wouldn't have to answer to anyone but herself. It was a scary thought being entirely on her own, but it was exhilarating too. After eighteen years of being everything her parents wanted her to be, she'd finally be free to be herself.

"And it's not so hard cooking for yourself," Dash continued. "Actually, I go out for a slice of pizza most of the time."

Lauren held up a hand to stop him. "You don't have to sell me," she said. "I'll do it."

Dash looked at her, surprised. "That's it?" he asked. "You don't even want to think about it?"

"I already have," Lauren said, "and it's the only solution. If I can sell the rest of my dorm contract and meal plan, I'll rent a room immediately. In fact, the more I think about it, the more it seems necessary to my career. All the great writers lived in freezing garrets, warming their hands over wood stoves, pinching pennies while they worked on their novels."

"It's not going to be *that* bad," Dash said.

"No, I'm saying I don't care how bad it gets. It's just one more experience I can write about later on. How can I write about life when I only know about being rich?"

"And it's cheaper," Dash reminded her. "I just wish there were some other way around your problem."

"It's not a problem any more," Lauren said,

gathering her papers and her calculator and throwing them in her knapsack. "It's going to be great." She leaned over and planted a kiss on Dash's lips. Then she slung her knapsack over her shoulder and headed for the door.

Three

....

"**W**hy am I doing this?" Faith panted the next day as she struggled to keep up with her next door neighbor, Kimberly Dayton, and Winnie. The three of them were exercising by running along the campus paths. "I thought this would take my mind off my worries, and instead I get something *new* to worry about—how out of shape I am!"

The warm, spring air felt hot on Faith's flushed skin. Every so often, a cool, piney breeze would come down from the mountains, but not often enough. The sweet smell of cherry blossoms beckoned the girls toward McLaren Plaza, a red brick square dotted with cherry trees. It would have been a beautiful day—if Faith were standing still.

Winnie's compact, muscular legs, clad in purple Lycra tights, pumped evenly. The rest of her was almost lost in her oversize Mickey Mouse sweatshirt. "You can do it!" Winnie encouraged Faith. "Why don't we sing to take our minds off the pain? *We're off to see the Wizard,*" she began at the top of her lungs.

Kimberly, a tall freshman who lived next door to Faith in Coleridge Hall sang along as she took loping strides with her lean legs. Her red tank unitard hugged her lithe dancer's body, while dozens of silver bracelets jangled on her arm as she ran.

Faith barely had enough breath to keep going, let alone sing. Maybe she should have said yes more often when Winnie asked her along on one of these fitness runs. But that was the least of Faith's problems. Right now her main concern was what she was going to do without Lauren.

Spring term had been going so well until Lauren had come home last night from Dash's apartment and told her she was leaving. And no matter how hard Faith had tried to talk her out of it, Lauren wouldn't listen. Faith understood that Lauren had money problems, but there had to be some other solution besides moving off campus.

Faith was determined to think of something. Just the thought of Lauren leaving gave her an empty feeling inside. Who would she talk to as she was falling asleep? Who would listen as seriously to her theater directing ideas and offer such thoughtful suggestions? Some other girl might buy Lauren's dorm contract and move in, but she could never replace her.

Now all Faith could do was hope someone would magically come along and rescue Lauren before she had to move.

Winnie and Kimberly slowed to a walk as they reached the cobbled brick plaza, and Faith sighed in gratitude. At least now she could stop worrying that her heart was going to fall out of her chest.

"Let's stretch!" Winnie said, leading the others toward the broad concrete steps of the Political Science building. She hopped up on the bottom step and hung her heels off the back to stretch her hamstring muscles. Kimberly propped one leg impossibly high on a stone wall and leaned over it with one arm above her head in a graceful curve. Faith plopped down in the nearby grass, under the shade of a cherry tree and watched as

Kimberly lowered her leg from the wall and eased herself into a split on the warm pavement.

"That's amazing," Faith said. "You're like a human rubberband."

Kimberly shifted around so she was in a straddle and lay her torso flat on the pavement.

"Oh, please," Faith said. "Don't show off unless you're planning to audition for my show."

That had been the other reason Faith had agreed to come on the run. Every time she'd brought up the audition, Kimberly had changed the subject or been on her way out the door. Now Faith had Kimberly cornered, and she wasn't going to take no for an answer.

One of the musical numbers Faith had chosen for her segment of the Follies was a solo song and dance routine. Kimberly would be just perfect for it, with her fluid, graceful movements and her clear, lyrical voice. Faith also had to admit that she would probably depend more on her friendship with Kimberly if Lauren really did move off campus.

"What show?" Kimberly asked as she lay comfortably on the ground in a perfect T-shape.

"Don't tell me you've forgotten already," Faith said. "I mentioned it to you this morning. And there are notices up in all the performing arts buildings and dance studios. The U. of S. Follies."

Kimberly pushed her torso up off the ground and brought her legs together. "I guess I didn't notice," she said, shrugging.

"Well, *you've* been noticed," Faith said. "All the directors have their eyes on you, especially since word has gotten out that you can sing. There aren't too many people on campus who can sing and dance as well as you can. But I want you to promise me you'll audition for me and no one else."

"There's one thing I don't understand," Winnie said, jumping off the step and lunging forward on one leg. "How can there be more than one director? It's just one show."

Faith rolled over onto her side and started running her palms lightly along the cool grass. "The production is always put together in such a hurry that there's no time for one director to do the whole thing. So Merideth, he's the junior in charge, has divided up the two-hour show into eight fifteen-minute segments. Each segment has a different director, and we can do whatever we want with our segment."

"What are you going to do?" Winnie asked, switching legs and lunging forward again.

"Four musical numbers in different styles.

One's going to be a love duet, one's a chorus line dance number, one's a patter song, and the one I want Kimberly for is a solo song and dance. I've chosen "When I Hear the Music" from that old 1930s musical *She's My Baby.*"

"Didn't Betty Boop sing that in a cartoon?" Kimberly asked. "I think I remember it from Saturday mornings. *'When I hear the music, it does something to me . . .'*" she sang in a sweet, unaffected soprano.

"That's it!" Faith said, pushing herself up to her knees. "See! You already know it!"

Kimberly shook her head. "Sorry, Faith. I'm really flattered that you asked me, but I don't think I'm the Betty Boop type."

"That was just one version of the song," Faith insisted. "You can sing it any way you want! At least say you'll come to the audition."

"Go for it, Kimberly!" Winnie said, hopping off the step and sitting beside Faith. "You have a nice voice. And I'll bet no one can do a split the way you can."

"I don't know," Kimberly mused. "I'm so busy taking dance classes, not to mention all my regular classes. Being in a show would be a big responsibility."

"Not this show!" Faith said. "We slap the whole thing together in less than two weeks, then it's over! And you'd only have to rehearse one number."

Kimberly crossed her ankles, Indian style, and leaned forward over her feet, stretching her back.

"All the dance majors I know are dying to get in," Faith said. "It's in the University Theater and everyone on campus goes to see it. It could help get you noticed as a dancer."

Kimberly hung forward a little more until her head was practically touching the ground.

"Please," Faith begged, leaning forward in the grass. "Just say you'll audition. It really means a lot to me right now to have my friends around. You'd be doing me a big favor."

Kimberly sighed and gracefully raised her head. "I guess it wouldn't hurt to just audition," she said.

"Yay!" Winnie cheered, clapping her hands.

Faith jumped up and gave her friend a hug.

"But don't play favorites," Kimberly warned. "Just because I'm your friend is no reason to give me the part."

Winnie couldn't wait to get back from her run. She couldn't wait to see her dorm again. It wasn't because Forest Hall was beautiful. The sterile cluster of buildings looked more like motels than examples of collegiate architecture. It wasn't because Forest Hall was so peaceful, either. Loud rock music blared out the open windows and crushed beer cans littered the front lawn.

Winnie couldn't wait to get back to Forest Hall because Josh Gaffey lived there too—right on her floor. Every time Winnie walked in the door, she had a chance of running into him. One of those times, she really *was* going to throw herself on top of him, if that's what it took to get him to sit down and finally talk things out with her.

Winnie skidded down the hill to the entrance and tripped over the beer cans in her rush to get inside. Then she pushed open the glass doors.

Whoopwhoopwhoopwhoop!

Winnie heard a whipping, whizzing sound and saw something hot pink sail through the air toward her.

"Aaaah!" she screamed, ducking down as the soft, spongy Turbofootball flew over her head into the beefy hands of a junior, Eric Bitterman. The hand that wasn't holding the football held a bottle of beer.

"All right!" Eric shouted. He was tall and muscular, with olive skin, short, dark curly hair, and brown eyes.

"Yo, Eric!" Steve beckoned from across the

lobby. Steve, even taller and brawnier than Eric, had long, shaggy, blond hair. He wore a T-shirt that said "Hang Ten" and was taking long swigs from a beer bottle. "Come on! It's time!" Steve said.

"Whooooa!" Eric said, laughing. "Par-ty! Par-ty! Par-ty!" He rushed by Winnie and ran down the hall after Steve.

Rolling her eyes, Winnie headed for the staircase leading up to her floor. Screams of laughing water balloon throwers echoed in the stairwell over the strains of a heavy metal guitar riff. But as soon as Winnie emerged onto her floor, all the noise seemed to die away instantly. The upstairs hall was full of people, yet she only saw one person, who was standing right in front of her door. Winnie caught her breath as he turned to face her. He was tall and slim, with dark hair reaching nearly to the collar of his baggy, untucked T-shirt. He wore faded jeans, a tiny earring in one ear, and a woven, leather bracelet around his wrist. Just looking at him filled Winnie with a hunger she was afraid could never be satisfied. It was Josh.

For a moment, they just stared at each other, oblivious to the soccer ball rolling down the hall between them. Then Josh's whole face lit up and he smiled his slightly lopsided grin. "You're home," he said. "I was hoping you'd show up soon."

"I'm glad I did!" Winnie smiled, bounding across the beige linoleum floor and impulsively throwing her arms around him. To her delight, he hugged her back, hard.

"That feels good," he murmured into her hair.

Winnie wanted to hang onto Josh forever. She wanted to burrow inside him so they'd never be separated again. She was afraid if she let go, he'd disappear again into the black hole of a Computer Center that had swallowed him up the past few weeks.

When they finally broke apart, Winnie looked up at him. "Well, I guess you've got to rush off somewhere, right? Catch you on the rebound."

"I know it's been hard for us to get together while I'm doing this research paper," Josh said, "but guess what? I've got a whole hour before my dad comes to take me home for the weekend. Do you want to talk?"

Winnie couldn't believe her luck. "Yes!" she cried. "We can talk in my room." Winnie unfastened her room key from the safety pin attached to her Mickey Mouse sweatshirt, and with nervous, excited fingers, she turned the key and pushed open her door.

"Oh, no," Winnie moaned. Her roommate,

Melissa McDormand, and Melissa's boyfriend, Brooks Baldwin, were on Melissa's bed, studying. Melissa's red hair fell over her freckled face as she lay on her stomach, leaning over her Organic Chemistry textbook. Brooks lay on his side, his face just inches away from Melissa's, reading a novel which was propped up on her back.

Melissa looked up at Winnie. "We were just leaving."

"Yeah," Brooks said, snapping his book shut and hopping off the bed. "We were on our way to my room to study."

Winnie stared at them for a second, open-mouthed. Until recently, Winnie hadn't had any privacy because Brooks and Melissa were always in the room. But when Winnie had finally lost her patience and told the two of them how she felt, they had promised to be more considerate. Now they were actually leaving so Winnie could be alone with Josh. Being assertive had really worked. "Thanks!" Winnie said.

"No problem," Brooks answered as he and Melissa filed out the doorway past Winnie and Josh. "See ya!"

As Brooks and Melissa walked off, Winnie turned to face Josh. Her heart started jumping around inside her chest and she was finding it difficult to breathe. The moment of truth had finally arrived. Winnie just hoped she could face the truth, whatever it happened to be.

"Come in," she said, trying to smile despite her nervousness. Josh ambled through the door and stood awkwardly in the center of the room, surrounded by the mess Winnie usually left there: her jingle bell boots, several pairs of running tights, a crumpled T-shirt, candy wrappers, old magazines, and a notebook she kept on the floor by her bed just in case she came up with any great ideas in the middle of the night and wanted to scribble them down.

Winnie shut the door and stood facing Josh. "Let's sit," she said, kicking aside the mess on the floor and perching nervously on the edge of her bed. Josh followed and sat beside her, not too close, but close enough for Winnie to smell the musky scent of his aftershave. She was dying to lean toward his neck and breathe it in. But they had to talk first. Funny, after waiting so long for this opportunity, Winnie didn't know where to begin, but her mouth started working anyway.

"You know, it's such an incredible coincidence that you only have an hour 'til you have to leave," Winnie chattered, " 'cause that's exactly the same amount of time I have until I have to go work at the Crisis Hot Line. But maybe it was more than a coincidence that your hour and my hour happened to be the same hour. I mean do you think maybe it was fate?"

Josh didn't answer. He just stared at Winnie with a stricken expression on his face. "What did you say?" he asked.

Winnie knew why Josh looked so shocked. He and Winnie hadn't spoken much since their break-up, so he didn't know that Winnie had started volunteering at the Crisis Hot Line—not to mention answered his call. Winnie giggled nervously. She wanted to tell him, but she didn't know how he would react. "You know," she said, "I wasn't really listening to myself while I was talking, which is probably what everyone else does, 'cause I'm such a motormouth. So what did I say?"

Josh rapidly shook his head. "I just wanted to know if I'd heard you correctly when you said you were working at the Crisis Hot Line. Is that true?"

Winnie swallowed hard and nodded. "I guess we've got a lot of catching up to do," she said. Unable to look Josh in the eye, she glanced down at the bedspread and noticed Josh's long, tapering fingers drumming silently against the bedspread. "A lot has happened since we broke up."

"So it seems," Josh said in a husky voice. Winnie felt her eyes being dragged upward again as she caught him staring at her with the same kind of hunger she was feeling. Oh why couldn't they forget words and simply devour each other? Wouldn't that really accomplish the same thing? Then they could get past the awkwardness and go back to just loving each other.

Winnie took a deep breath and slid a little closer to Josh. He sat, motionless, waiting, his brown eyes unblinking as he stared at her. He was breathing rapidly and Winnie could almost feel his heart pounding, as rapidly as hers. Winnie slid even closer until she could feel the warmth of his body engulf her. At the same moment she tilted her face upward, he bent toward her and . . .

Crash! It sounded like someone was trying to break the door down. There was a loud scream outside the hallway, then an insistent knocking on the door. Winnie didn't want to lose the moment with Josh, but maybe someone was in trouble. Winnie opened the door.

Steve Powell, Eric Bitterman, and Dave Baker, a hockey player, tumbled into the room, laughing hysterically.

"Did you see that?" Steve yelled. "That girl was so scared! She thought it was 'The Blob' coming out of the toilet."

Winnie peered out at the open bathroom door across the hall and felt her stomach convulse in disgust. Green slime oozed out from under each of the toilet stalls and posters of Freddy Krueger in his hockey mask covered the windows.

"You're a genius, that's what you are," Eric said, pounding Steve on the back. "A certifiable genius."

"What is going on here?" Winnie asked, putting her hands on her hips.

Dave, a sturdy-looking guy with straight, light brown hair, a long, thin nose, and a moustache, imitated Winnie's pose. "What is going on here?" he sang in a falsetto voice.

"We're having a party!" Eric said. "And we're serving Jell-O!"

All three jocks laughed hysterically.

"Could you guys take this out in the hall?" Josh asked, trying to usher them toward the door.

"I don't think so," Eric said. "The young lady asked us a question, and I think it's our duty, as gentlemen and scholars, to give her an answer." Eric wrapped his arm around Steve's shoulder. "This young man," he said, "this incredibly brilliant, young man, has just pulled off the most incredibly brilliant stunt I've ever seen. He redecorated the girls' bathroom and filled the toilets with Jell-O. Is that incredibly brilliant, or what?"

"Now, look, you guys, I'm sure you're really funny," Winnie said without humor, "but we're trying . . ."

"Yo, Steve," a voice called from out in the hall. "What do you want me to do with this one?"

Another tall, beefy, drunken jock whom Winnie didn't recognize staggered through the doorway carrying a bucket, sloshing with not-yet-congealed orange Jell-O.

"Please!" Winnie begged. "Not in here!"

But before the words had left her mouth, the jock tripped over Winnie's jingle bell boots and spilled the watery, orange goo all over the floor. The jock slid on the Jell-O and fell on Winnie's bed, still holding the sticky bucket.

Winnie gave Josh an anguished look. In just forty-eight minutes, he would be leaving for the entire weekend. They'd never get the room cleaned up before then. Their moment was more than lost—their moment had been destroyed in a Jell-O explosion!

Four

he china dishes were rimmed with gold, and the sterling silverware had an engraved pattern of tiny, raised bows connected by swirls of ribbon. KC's fork felt heavy and smooth in her hand as she delicately speared a tiny, new potato and brought it to her mouth. As she chewed, she sighed. It felt so natural to be in the formal Tri Beta dining room with its mahogany table covered by a pure white, linen cloth.

KC had never felt this comfortable in her parents' health food restaurant, The Windchime. She'd always felt out of place at the roughhewn wooden tables with their hard, wooden benches carved with the customers' initials. She'd never liked the mushy vegetable concoctions that her mother served in handmade crockery. She'd always felt like she'd been born into the wrong family. But tonight, KC felt like she'd finally come home.

"More roast beef, KC?" asked Sarah Mills, a freshman Tri Beta sister who sat to KC's right.

Sarah held a gold-rimmed platter heaped with steaming slices of juicy, pink meat. Sarah, a San Francisco debutante, wore a powder-blue, cashmere sweaterdress decorated only with a simple strand of pearls. Her straight, brown hair was pulled back with a powder blue and pink headband.

"Thank you," KC said, helping herself to a piece of roast beef while Sarah held the platter. Then KC took the platter and offered it to president Courtney Conner, who sat to her left at the head of the long table. A few weeks ago, KC might have secretly gloated that she, a newcomer and member of a family that had never heard of the Social Register, let alone been in it, had become such good friends with the president of the most prestigious sorority on campus. But now she just felt glad to have her friend nearby.

"More roast beef?" KC asked Courtney.

Courtney shook her head, making her shoulder-length blond hair swing loosely around her face. She wore a deep mauve silk blouse with a long, colorful, ethnic print skirt. While Courtney's outfit was expensive and in the best of taste, KC also realized how much Courtney's style had changed since meeting Phoenix Cates. Phoenix, a freshman Courtney had met while spending a few days in the hospital for a mild concussion, was probably even more of a flower child than KC's parents!

"I'd love some more roast beef," Courtney said, "but what would Phoenix say? He'd make me feel guilty about the poor, sad-eyed cow who gave her life for this meal."

"The cow didn't die in vain," KC said. "This meat is delicious."

Courtney pushed back her heavy chair with its cream-colored silk cushions that matched the cream-colored silk wallpaper. "I've got to do my presidential thing now," she said, winking at KC and gracefully rising to her feet.

The elegantly dressed Tri Beta sisters grew silent. Two dozen pretty faces, enhanced by velvet headbands, pearls, gold earrings, or heirloom cameo pins, turned expectantly to the head of the table.

Courtney smiled at her sisters. "Hi," she said

simply. "Keep eating. Just think of me as part of your dinner entertainment."

Everyone laughed and Courtney grinned, two things that had also never happened before Courtney met Phoenix. He was a free spirit whose relaxed and carefree attitude about life had rubbed off on Courtney. So when Marielle's spiteful photos of the two of them swimming in their underwear in Hosmer Lake had gotten around campus, Courtney had realized that she didn't want to deny any part of who she was anymore. She'd stopped acting prim and proper, and her popularity had climbed even higher, both in and out of the sorority house.

"I'll make this brief," Courtney said, "because we've got an extra-special dessert tonight in honor of our new pledges, and *I,* for one, can't wait!"

Courtney leaned forward and rested her fingertips lightly on the white linen tablecloth. "First of all," she said, "I'd like to welcome all our new sisters to the Tri Beta family—and I mean that literally. We are like a family. Even though Tri Betas don't actually live here until their sophomore year, I want you all to think of this house as your home until you graduate.

"Tri Beta is and should be a place where you'll find support, no matter what you're going through; a place where you can take off your shoes and have fun. And most of all, a place where you'll form friendships that will last the rest of your life."

There was a murmuring around the table and approving glances as girls broke into smiles.

With one hand, Courtney brushed back a smooth lock of blond hair that had fallen forward over her face. "Of course it's not going to be all fun and games," she said with a slightly more serious expression. "We still have rules. For instance, you are all expected to attend Tri Beta activities such as these weekly Monday dinners."

"Eat this delicious food *every week?*" freshman Marcia Tabbert joked. "Please, Courtney. Say it isn't so!"

Courtney joined the laughter around the table. "Life is tough," she agreed. "Anyway, you'll receive a booklet outlining the rest of our events, but they include parties, charity functions, work sessions, and more. We've got one event coming up this Saturday, though, that I'd like to tell you about. It's a formal dance at the Gamma house where all new pledges will be presented to other Greeks on the row. Right before that, we'll have our own candlight ceremony here at the house."

"Is that the initiation ceremony?" KC asked.

Courtney shook her head. "That comes later,"

she said. "This is more like a welcome-to-the-club party."

"Do we bring dates?" asked Lisa Jean McDermott, a new pledge.

"You'll all need escorts," Courtney explained, "but not for our candlelight ceremony, just for the dance at Gamma. Have your dates meet you there, not here. Oh, and by the way, I know you're all gorgeous and desirable females who'd never have any problem getting a date, but if, by some fluke of fate, you just happen to be dateless that evening, come talk to me or Diane Woo, our secretary. We've got a little black book." Courtney grinned mischievously.

KC found herself grinning, too. Courtney was setting a new tone for Tri Beta that would make it even more desirable to be a member. And with nasty Marielle Danner banished from the sorority forever, it was going to be smooth sailing for the next three-and-a-half years. Marielle had been thrown out for getting KC drunk right before the Tri Beta tea at which KC was evaluated by the sisters. KC had made a fool of herself at the tea. Courtney, however, had forgiven KC when she learned Marielle had set her up.

That all seemed like a long time ago, now that KC was actually, finally a Tri Beta. And KC wasn't looking back. She was just looking forward to all of it—the parties, the dinners, and even the responsibilities. The only things she was worried about were keeping up her grades and finding an escort for the Gamma party.

There was only one place KC wanted to look —the ground floor of Coleridge Hall—home of Peter Dvorsky. But she couldn't help worrying how Peter would look to the other Tri Betas. He wasn't a hunk, he didn't play on any of the teams, and he certainly wasn't in a fraternity. On the face of him, there was nothing that might impress her sisters.

On the other hand, Peter might not even want to go to the dance with KC. He thought the whole Greek system was silly—just a bunch of snobs trying to impress each other with their money and judging other people by their appearance.

Yet KC wanted Peter to like her sorority as much as she wanted her sisters to like him. Succeeding as a Tri Beta was still all-important, but KC was no longer willing to give up everything and everyone else in her life for it. Was there a way to make both halves of her life work together?

Of course, if she didn't pull up her English grade with her extra credit paper, she wouldn't have to worry about Tri Beta, because she wouldn't be in it any longer. KC still hadn't found someone to help her on her English comp paper and it was due this coming Friday.

KC tried not to let her anxieties ruin her appetite as she ate rich, dark, chocolate mousse, but most of the dessert remained in the crystal bowl.

"KC?" Courtney asked gently, after the other girls had gone upstairs to start their homework.

"Hmmm?" KC looked up and noticed that she and Courtney were alone.

"Do you want to talk?" Courtney asked. "I've got a few minutes before I have to start my homework."

"I'd like that," KC said. She and Courtney rose from the table and went into the livingroom. It was a warm, elegant room with a marble-topped fireplace at one end and a cozy collection of plump sofas and matching armchairs. Blue and white floor-to-ceiling drapes were pulled back with silk-tasseled ties. Through the windows, KC could see the grassy front lawn, almost white in the moonlight.

Courtney sat down on one of the sofas and propped her long, slender legs on the coffee table. Then she kicked off her high heeled pumps. "So tell me," she said as KC settled into an armchair. "What's on your mind?"

"Well . . ." KC heaved a sigh and looked

down at her hands while she laced her fingers together. "I was just wondering who your escort will be for the Gamma dance. Or, maybe I should ask, which president of which fraternity will be your date?"

Courtney gave KC a questioning look. "You know who I'm bringing," she said.

"I do?" KC asked.

"Of course you do," Courtney answered with a dreamy smile. "Phoenix Cates!"

KC's jaw dropped open. She knew Courtney really liked the earthy, long-haired freshman with his Grateful Dead T-shirts and tattered jeans, but she couldn't believe Courtney would actually invite him to a fraternity party. It was even harder to imagine Phoenix on Greek Row than it was to imagine Peter there. Courtney was a junior and president of a sorority. Phoenix was an eighteen-year-old hippie freshman!

"Are you serious?" KC asked.

"Well, I wouldn't say we're serious, yet," Courtney said, "but we're certainly heading in that direction."

"No, I meant, are you serious about bringing him to the dance?"

"Oh. Of course! I thought that was understood."

"And you don't care that he's not a Greek?" KC asked, thinking not of Phoenix but of Peter.

"The only thing I care about is how I feel about him," Courtney said. "And how he makes me feel. When I'm with Phoenix, I'm so relaxed. I can really be myself with him. He's the only person I'd even think of bringing."

KC broke into a huge smile. Courtney hadn't realized it, but she had answered KC's real question. If Courtney could bring Phoenix to the dance, then KC could certainly invite Peter.

"Thank you!" KC said, coming around the coffee table to give Courtney a hug.

"For what?" Courtney asked.

"For not being afraid," KC said. "You're a good influence on me."

"Uh oh," Courtney said. "I was trying to go in the other direction. I've spent too many years being good." Courtney looked at her antique watch. "On the other hand, I don't want to be too bad either. I've got to start my homework."

"Yeah, me too," KC said, the pit in her stomach reminding her once again of her extra credit English paper. She retrieved her purse from the armchair and headed for the entrance hall.

"Speaking of homework," Courtney said as she followed KC to the front door, "how are your classes? Not too hard, I hope?"

"They're fine," KC said in a neutral voice.

"That's good," Courtney said. "I guess you're not having any trouble meeting the academic standards here at Tri Beta." She smiled as if to show how little she was worried about KC.

KC spread her lips into a natural-looking smile. "I'm a Tri Beta," she said in a proud voice, "and I'm here to stay."

Courtney squeezed KC's arm. "Good," she said warmly. "Well, I'll see you tomorrow."

KC gave Courtney a quick peck on the cheek and opened the front door to the clear, starry night. After the door had closed behind her, she turned back to look at the Tri Beta house, an elegant three-storied colonial with tall columns on either side of the door and a widow's walk on top. Golden light poured out of the upstairs windows. This was her home now and nothing was going to keep her out of it, not spiteful Marielle, and certainly not bad grades. Whatever it took to bring up her average, KC was going to do it. She checked her watch. It was seven o'clock. There was still an hour left before the campus offices that were still open closed. KC knew exactly which one to head toward.

"Let me guess," said the young man sitting behind the desk at the Learning Center. He was thin and balding, and he smiled at KC. "You need a tutor."

"Is it that obvious?" KC asked. Was her problem really this transparent? That meant Courtney and all the other Tri Betas had seen it, too.

The young man laughed. "No," he said. "But that's why people come here."

"Oh!" KC relaxed. "I'm sorry. I don't know why I'm so nervous."

"Everyone's nervous their first time. It's a big step." He laughed again. "I'm Richard Krasnoff, and I'm in the Masters teaching program. Have a seat and tell me what you're looking for."

Lowering herself into a brown folding chair by the desk, KC squinted from the harsh fluorescent lights that buzzed up near the ceiling. The small, cinderblock room was drab and bare except for a bulletin board covering one wall. On it were neat columns of index cards labeled "Tutor Wanted" with names and phone numbers of other students. Well, if they could go public, so could she —as long as no one from Tri Beta found out.

KC introduced herself and explained her problem. "It's English," she said. "I don't have trouble speaking it or writing grammatical sentences, but for some reason I have trouble writing papers. The thoughts just swirl in my head and I can't seem to write them down in any sort of logical order. And now I've got to write a persuasive essay for English comp, and I'm panicking."

"I see," Richard said, nodding his head. "You need help organizing your ideas."

"Exactly," KC said. "Can you help me?"

"Oh, no," Richard said, "I don't tutor. I just refer you. But I think I know the perfect person to help you." Richard riffled through a looseleaf binder on his desk and stopped when he got to a certain page. "Ah, yes," he said, reading from the binder. "Sheldon Copperstein. Sophomore. Government major. On the debating team." Richard looked up from the page. "I've heard he can argue both sides of an argument and persuade you he's right both times. How's that for persuasive?"

"Sounds good," KC said hopefully.

"And he's super-organized," Richard said. "This guy alphabetizes the wrappers that the stamps in his stamp collection come in."

"That is organized," KC agreed, though she was beginning to wonder what kind of nerd Sheldon Copperstein was. KC pictured him in his room, hunched over his stamps, a skinny, pimply young man with thick glasses. But it didn't matter what he looked like. KC needed help, and if Sheldon could work wonders, who was she to make fun of him? "How do I get in touch with him?" KC asked.

"I'll call him right now and see if he's available," Richard said. "He lives in Baker House, the guys-only study dorm."

"Oh, great," KC said. "I'm in Langston. That's right next door."

Richard nodded as he picked up the phone to dial. "Good," he said. "Then you won't need to come here for your session. You guys can get together in the dorm." Richard punched in Sheldon's number and waited while it rang. "I'm sure he's home," Richard said. "He's always home . . . Hello, Sheldon? It's Richard over at the Learning Center . . . Oh, I'm sorry to disturb you . . ." Richard covered the mouthpiece with his hand and smiled conspiratorially at KC. "Sheldon's dusting his stamp collection," he whispered. "Uh, yes, I'm still here," he said, speaking into the phone again. "I have a young lady here who needs a tutor in English. Are you available?" Richard gave KC the thumbs up sign. "On Wednesday?" He covered the mouthpiece again. "Is that soon enough?"

KC nodded. "The paper's not due 'til next Monday. I think that should be okay."

Richard hung up the phone a moment later. "Sheldon says to meet him in his room on

Wednesday at seven. I'll write down the info for you."

KC's heart filled with joy and relief. *Sheldon Copperstein,* she thought, *I don't care what you look like. You're my savior!*

Five

Tuesday afternoon, Lauren found herself standing in front of a red brick apartment building. It was narrow, four stories tall, sandwiched between a burnt-out warehouse and a pawnshop. Stenciled on the weatherworn front door, in peeling gold paint, were the numbers "111."

"One eleven Neptune Avenue," Lauren read the numbers aloud, checking the address against the one she'd written on a scrap of paper. "My new home."

She hadn't even seen the apartment yet, but Lauren knew she was going to love it. It was affordable, it was within walking distance of school, and it was going to be her first real home as an independent adult. What more could she ask for? Lauren had to smile at how quickly her life had turned around. A few days after deciding to move off campus, she'd seen the ad for this room. It had to be fate.

There was a brisk clicking of heels against pavement. Lauren turned to see Kimberly, tall and regal in her long, black raincoat, rushing down the sidewalk toward her. Kimberly wore a colorful, silk scarf wrapped around her head, and huge, dangly, silver hoops.

"So!" Kimberly said. "Is this it?"

"This is it," Lauren said, gesturing grandly to the building. "I'm so glad you could come." Winnie, Dash, and KC all had classes and Faith was setting up for her auditions the next day, but Lauren was glad that at least one of her friends was here to give her a second opinion. She was starting a whole new life and she wanted everything to be perfect.

"What do we do now?" Kimberly asked.

There was a rusty intercom panel outside the front door with eight buttons and a speaker. Lauren pressed one of the buttons and waited.

"Who is it?" squawked a metallic voice.

"Lauren Turnbell-Smythe," Lauren answered.

A loud buzzer sounded and Lauren pushed the

front door open. Kimberly followed, and the girls found themselves in a narrow hallway with a staircase at the back. In the middle of the hall, facing each other, were two green doors. Kimberly instantly noticed that each door had several locks on it. One even had a sign: Beware of Dog.

"Not bad, huh?" Lauren asked, turning back to give Kimberly a smile. She started trudging up the stairs. "And it's on the fourth floor, so I'll get plenty of exercise."

"Sure saves time going to the gym," Kimberly agreed, climbing the stairs behind Lauren. The stair railing was thick and shiny from its many layers of paint, and the walls, too, looked like they had been painted over often.

As Lauren rounded the corner on the first landing, she wiped the sweat off her forehead. "I feel like I'm losing weight already!" she said cheerfully.

Kimberly said nothing.

When they finally reached the top floor, Lauren stopped to catch her breath, then knocked on the door of apartment 4R.

"Who is it?" called a suspicious-sounding female voice.

"Lauren Turnbell-Smythe," Lauren said again. "I spoke to you earlier about the room?"

The door opened a crack with a chain still

across the opening. Beneath the chain, a pair of eyes peered out from a wrinkled face. Then the chain slid back with a squeak of metal, and the door opened.

"Come in!" said the tiny lady in the doorway. Her gray hair was short and fluffy, and her arms and legs were thin. She wore a faded housedress with a blazer over it.

"Mrs. Calvin?" Lauren asked politely. "I believe I spoke to you on the phone?"

"I spoke to a lot of people," Mrs. Calvin said, waving her hand dismissively.

"Is this your apartment?" Lauren asked.

"No," Mrs. Calvin said. "My grandson owns the building. I just watch over it for him. You want to look around?"

Lauren nodded eagerly and stepped inside. Kimberly, too, entered the room.

It was small, but it was cozy. The living part of the room was about eight by ten feet with two small windows facing onto a brick wall. A single light fixture in the ceiling held a single lightbulb. The wooden floor was dark and unpolished.

About the same size as the living area was a kitchen space, with a cracked linoleum floor. There were a few cabinets, attached to the wall at varying heights, a stained porcelain sink, and a refrigerator with a puddle of water under it. A new stove, with the labels still attached, had been jammed between the sink and the refrigerator.

"Look, Kimberly!" Lauren said excitedly. "A new stove!"

"Great," Kimberly said as she sidestepped the puddle so she could admire the stove with Lauren.

"We fix it up nice!" Mrs. Calvin agreed. "Only the best. The bathroom's over there," she said, pointing to a door in the back wall of the kitchen.

"The bathroom seems pretty good," Lauren said, as she and Kimberly looked inside. An old porcelain bathtub with a rusty chain and rubber stopper hanging over the side filled most of the room. Lauren had always loved old-fashioned bathtubs. This one even had clawed feet! A toilet was squeezed between the bathtub and the wall. A pedestal sink stood at the end of the bathtub, leaving a small space to move around in.

Lauren was charmed. It wasn't a palace, but it had the most important thing: atmosphere. Lauren felt sure living in this funky place would inspire her creativity much more than living in the dorms.

"What's the rent?" Lauren asked Mrs. Calvin.

"Two twenty-five a month."

"Two hundred twenty-five dollars?" Lauren

asked with disbelief. The ad had said cheap, but this was even better than she'd expected. Lauren's instincts had been right. This was it! She had to have this apartment.

"Take it or leave it," Mrs. Calvin said. "If you don't want it, there are plenty of people who will."

"She could be bluffing," Kimberly whispered to Lauren.

"Oh no, I don't think so," Lauren said. "This is a really good deal. And it's even got a new stove!"

There was a loud buzzing sound, and Mrs. Calvin went to the intercom on the wall by the door. *"Who is it?"* she squawked. A metallic voice said something, and Mrs. Calvin pushed the button labeled "door." "More customers," she told Lauren and Kimberly.

"Oh no!" Lauren panicked as they heard the sound of footsteps on the stairs. "When they see this, they're going to take it away from me!"

"It's okay," Kimberly tried to calm her. "I'm sure there are plenty of other apartments around here."

"Not at this price," Lauren said. "And I can't afford to pay any more than this."

"What about your dorm contract?" Kimberly

argued. "You really shouldn't take an apartment until you sell it. You can't afford to pay for both."

"And I can't afford to pass this up," Lauren said as the footsteps approached the front door. Lauren pulled a wad of money out of her jacket pocket. "How much to hold the apartment?" she asked Mrs. Calvin.

"First month's rent plus one month security," Mrs. Calvin said.

As Lauren started counting out the bills, there was a knock on the door.

"Lauren!" Kimberly hissed. "That's $450! Don't you think you should look . . ."

Mrs. Calvin went to open the door.

"Don't answer it," Lauren said, pressing the money in Mrs. Calvin's hand. "I want this apartment!"

Mrs. Calvin nodded and stuffed the money in the pocket of her blazer. Then she opened the door a crack with the chain still on. "It's taken!" she shouted, slamming the door shut again.

Lauren turned to Kimberly with a triumphant look on her face. "It's mine!" she said. "My very own place! And I got it with my own money, without any help from anyone. Except you, of course."

Kimberly smiled. "That's great, Lauren."

"When can I move in?" Lauren asked Mrs. Calvin.

Mrs. Calvin shrugged. "It's empty, isn't it?"

"Great!" Lauren exclaimed. "Oh, and by the way," she said in a very grown-up voice, "I'd like a receipt, please."

"If my mother could see me now," Lauren sighed happily as she and Kimberly passed an empty lot choked with weeds.

It's a good thing she can't, Kimberly thought to herself as she checked over her shoulder for the thirtieth time. Kimberly knew Lauren's mother had cut Lauren off completely, but no mother would want her daughter living in this neighborhood, even if they weren't speaking to each other.

"All my life she's told me what to do, who to be friends with, how to dress, how to *be,*" Lauren rambled on, seemingly oblivious to her surroundings. "Now I'm completely on my own, and I *love* it!"

The girls crossed the street to a block with a neat row of shops and well-kept brownstones. They were nearing the campus. Kimberly started to relax.

"There's something to be said for independence," Kimberly agreed. "Not that I'd know what that feels like—yet."

Lauren looked at Kimberly with interest. "Do you have a domineering mother, too?"

Kimberly shrugged. "Well—I wouldn't call her domineering, exactly, but she's a very strong person."

"I know she runs the Houston Modern Dance Company," Lauren said. "It must take a lot of will and determination to be in charge of a company that big."

"Definitely," Kimberly said. "She's got plenty of both. She's got to be business manager, artistic director, teacher, choreographer, and mother to about fifty dancers, many of whom can't or don't want to think for themselves. Sometimes I wonder if she lumps me in with the rest of them."

"I'm sure she knows which one is her daughter," Lauren said as they passed a sidewalk café filled with students drinking coffee and eating pastries.

"Yes and no," Kimberly said. "I mean, she's really been a wonderful mother to me, very caring and understanding, like a friend as well as a mom. But sometimes I feel like she expects certain things of me, without asking me if they're what *I* want."

"I know how that is," Lauren said.

"She expects me to be a dancer, for one thing."

"Wait a minute," Lauren said, stopping short on the sidewalk. "Do you mean to tell me that you, Miss Dancer with the legwarmers and the mile-long legs that are the envy of everyone in Coleridge Hall, don't want to be a dancer?"

Kimberly hadn't planned to spill that little secret to anybody. She'd hardly admitted it to herself yet. But the truth was, after thirteen years of studying at her mother's school, after nearly a lifetime of planning, *expecting* to be a dancer, Kimberly was beginning to doubt if that's what she really wanted.

It wasn't that she didn't enjoy dancing or that she wasn't talented. Kimberly loved taking class and working on placement and perfecting her technique. But the thought of performing in front of an audience had always terrified her. Her mother had always said it was just stagefright, but Kimberly knew it was much, much worse. Each year, when she got under the glaring lights at her mother's annual school recital, with all those eyes watching her, Kimberly's mind would fill with irrational fears: fear the scenery would fall on her, fear she'd trip and break her leg, fear the stage would open up and swallow her.

Of course none of these things ever happened, but that didn't make it any easier. If anything, her fears were getting worse as she got older. And now with Faith bugging her to audition for the U. of S. Follies, Kimberly had begun to feel those crazy fears even when she wasn't on stage.

But no one could know this, especially not Faith. It was Kimberly's problem, and Kimberly was going to work it out.

Kimberly tugged nervously at the colorful, silk scarf tied around her head. "I just have a little problem with stagefright," Kimberly said. "When I get up in front of an audience, I sort of clam up."

"Faith did mention she had to practically use brute force to get you to audition for the Follies," Lauren said.

"Was it that noticeable?" Kimberly worried. "I didn't want her to think I don't care about her show." *Especially now that her roommate is abandoning her and she feels so alone,* Kimberly wanted to add. She knew Faith sincerely wanted her to audition for the Follies. But she also knew that Faith wanted to have her friends around her now that Lauren was moving off campus.

"Then show her you care," Lauren suggested. "Just show up at the audition. You don't have to be in it if you don't want to. You might not even get the part."

"That's true," Kimberly said. "And I guess sometimes you've got to put your friends ahead of your fears."

Six

 lick!

"More eyes. Bigger. Wider. Come on, let's see those baby grays."

Click!

"Now pout for me. Give me those full lips. No, not like you're kissing, like you're upset. Get mad at me, steaming mad. Remember the time I threw you in Mill Pond?"

Click! Click! Click!

"That's it, KC. You're beautiful when you're angry!"

While Lauren and Kimberly were walking back to campus, Peter was peering through his viewfinder and laughing as KC stuck out her tongue at him. He had posed her next to a cast-iron statue of Derwood C. Brock, the founding president of U. of S. For once, KC wasn't wearing one of her dress-for-success pleated skirts and blazers. Peter had convinced her to wear a simple, white T-shirt and jeans for this photo shoot. He moved in closer and refocused the lens until her face was nearly filling the frame.

"Okay, have it your way," Peter said as he took a picture of KC with her tongue sticking out, "but don't blame me if this one ends up in the series. It certainly shows another side of you."

"Peter!" KC exclaimed, horrified. "You wouldn't!"

"My photography assignment was to do a series of six portraits showing different sides of one person. I'm just following directions."

"You can follow those directions right out of here if you use that one," KC said. "Promise me you won't."

"Oh, that's right," Peter said, lowering his camera for a moment and grinning wickedly at KC. "You have your image to maintain, now that you're a Tri Beta."

KC's expression became as chilly as the one on the iron face of President Brock. She turned her head and looked off in the direction of the cherry trees bordering McLaren Plaza, ignoring Peter and ignoring the crowd of students who had gathered to watch them play at photographer and model.

In profile, KC's face was even more lovely than it was head-on. Her long, straight nose was haughty and fragile at the same time. Her cool, gray eyes, rimmed with thick, black lashes, seemed to give off light, not just reflect it. Her lush, generous lips and thick, dark hair added a sensuous softness to her translucent skin.

Click! Click! Click!

Peter snapped away as KC turned back to face him. "Okay," she admitted, her expression growing softer, "maybe I am too concerned about my image. But with all the pictures you're taking, I'm sure you could find six that don't include me sticking out my tongue!"

"We'll have to see," Peter said nonchalantly. "I'm going to choose these shots solely on the basis of artistic merit."

"Oh, brother," KC said, lounging back against the cast-iron feet of President Brock. Her long, slender body made a gently curving line at the base of the statue, echoing the curve of the distant mountaintops. Peter moved back a few feet so he could get KC and the mountains in the same frame. He couldn't decide which of the two stunning examples of natural beauty was more breathtaking.

Click! Click! Beeeeeeeep!

"What's that?" KC asked in alarm. "Did I break the lens?"

"Hardly," Peter said, smiling. "My electronic camera's telling me I'm out of film. Hold on a minute while I reload." With shaking fingers, he ripped open a yellow box of film and fumbled with it as he tried to load it in the camera.

What was wrong with him? He'd photographed beautiful girls before. He'd even photographed KC before. So why did he feel so nervous at the sight of her smooth, white throat, delicately arched as she tilted her chin back? Why did he have the urge to fling his camera aside and scoop her up in his arms the way he had at Mill Pond a few weeks ago? Why couldn't he stop thinking about how her wet body had felt as he held her pressed against his bare chest?

"Peter?" KC asked. "Is something wrong?"

Peter looked down at his fumbling fingers and saw that the roll of film had fallen to the ground. He stooped to pick it up, keeping his head down. Still kneeling, he loaded the film into his camera and fiddled with the lens.

"Technical difficulties," he muttered. "We'll be up and running in just a minute."

"Is there anything I can do?" KC asked.

Peter shook his head. He was beginning to feel self-conscious, insecure, and scared. Scared he could really fall for her, after all these months of fighting it. Scared that once he showed her how he really felt, she'd dump him for a better looking guy the way she had for the Winter Formal. Either that, or she'd go running to her sorority sisters so they could all get a good laugh at how a guy like him had the nerve to be interested in someone like her. His only defense was not showing KC how much he cared.

"Oh, that's a nice one," Peter said sarcastically as he focused on KC's increasingly exasperated, impatient face. She looked like she was getting tired of waiting. "It's amazing what a range of expressions you have. Everything from disgruntled to annoyed. I'm sure I'm going to have a lot to choose from."

"How about this one?" KC said, puffing out her cheeks and crossing her eyes.

"I love it!" Peter said, snapping away. "And so will the Tri Betas."

"I know you won't show anything but *serious, artistic* poses," KC said, scrunching up her nose and furrowing her eyebrows.

Peter lowered his camera and waited. "Are you through?"

"How about this one?" KC said, swinging herself upright and jumping up next to the statue. "Oh, President Brock," she said seductively, squeezing the statue's arm. "I really admire a man with power. And your muscles are *so strong*. Like they're made of steel! Or at least iron."

"No flirting on my time," Peter teased. "Come down from there."

KC slung one arm across the statue's shoulder. "But Brocky and I are tired!" she complained. "You've already taken six rolls of pictures. How many do you need?"

"Okay, okay. Take a break," Peter said. He unslung the camera from around his neck and tucked it inside his black camera bag. Then he hefted up the bag and went to sit down on a bench in the plaza.

KC followed him and sat down beside him. With KC so near, Peter found it even more difficult to ignore the wet gleam of her lips, the smoothness of her skin, the shiny thickness of her hair. It was easier to be objective with the camera between them. Now, without it, he had to face the truth. He was hopelessly in love with her. Steeling his face, Peter stared straight ahead at the Political Science building.

"Don't be mad at me," KC said, shifting forward so that her face was in front of his. "I just need a few minutes, then I'll be a good model again."

"I'm not mad at you," Peter said stiffly.

"Then what's wrong?" KC asked.

Peter turned to look at her, trying to ignore her at the same time. "Nothing," he said pleasantly.

"Good," KC said. " 'Cause there was something I wanted to ask you."

"What?" Peter asked.

"It's not one of your favorite topics," KC said.

"I can't wait to hear it," Peter said.

"It's about my sorority."

"Let me guess," Peter said. "You need a photographer for your debutante ball with the Alpha Beta Gamma Deltas."

"Do you really hate sororities and fraternities so much?" KC asked, her eyes anxious.

"No," Peter said. "Actually, I don't care much about them one way or the other."

"Oh, good. I mean, I'm glad that at least you don't hate the Greeks, because there was something I wanted to ask you."

"So I've heard," Peter said. "Are you going to tell me today, or do you want to sleep on it?"

KC heaved a deep sigh. *Okay, Angeletti*, she said to herself. *Out with it.* Then she got up off the bench and scooted around behind it to a grassy area. Leaning down, she picked a dandelion, then stood up again. Peter watched her curiously.

"Mr. Dvorsky," KC said, leaning over the back of the bench and presenting him with the dandelion. "I know you have a very busy schedule, and I know you're not crazy about my new friends at Tri Beta, and I know you're probably going to say no, but . . . would you be my date to the Gamma party this Saturday night?"

Peter took the dandelion and stared at its yellow, pointed petals, unable to say a word.

KC gave herself a little slap on the side of the head. "Of course you don't know what to say. You probably don't even know what a Gamma party is! Well, it *is* a sorority party, but it's not as bad as it sounds. I mean, it's going to be a formal dance to introduce the new spring pledges to the rest of the sororities and fraternities, but you don't really have to dress up if you don't want to. You'll just need to wear a jacket and tie. There's also going to be lots of food, and you won't have to give up your whole evening because there's a candlelight ceremony earlier at Tri Beta which is just for us girls, so all you'd have to do is meet me at Gamma house." KC paused for breath. "Wow!" she exclaimed. "I sounded like Winnie just now!"

Peter still couldn't speak. He couldn't believe what he was hearing. Not only was KC inviting him to a party, not only was she asking him to be her date at a sorority function, but she actually seemed nervous about how he would answer!

"Okay, *don't* answer," KC said. "Don't even twitch a facial muscle to give me a hint whether your answer is yes or no. Are you always this cool and unimpressed when a girl asks you out on a date? Or do you already have a better offer for Saturday night?"

Cool? Peter felt about as cool as a hot tamale. His face felt flushed and his palms were sweating and his heart was trying to beat its way out of his chest. This had to be the greatest thing that had ever happened to him. KC Angeletti, movie star gorgeous, Freshman Princess, Tri Beta KC Angeletti, had asked him out! But her anxious look reminded him that he still hadn't answered.

"No, I don't have a better offer," he said finally. "I mean, *yes,* I'd be very happy to escort you to your party."

"You would?" KC asked, her mouth opening in surprise.

"What did you think I was going to say?" Peter asked.

"I had no idea what you were going to say."

"Well now you know," Peter said, daring to

take her slender hand in his. "I'd *love* to be your date."

KC looked up at him with such a look of happiness that Peter dared to go one step further. He wrapped his arms around her and pulled her toward him. Then he leaned over her until his lips were touching hers. He kept waiting for her to push him away, but she didn't. Her eyes closed, her lips parted, and she pressed her body against his as she kissed him back.

Seven

hen I hear the music, it does something to me . . ."

"Oh no! I forgot my base! I can't go up on that stage without my base. I'll look as white as a ghost!"

"One two three kick, step kick, turn turn . . ."

As Faith tried to get inside the crowded lobby of the University Theater Wednesday morning, she couldn't believe how many people had turned up to audition for the U. of S. Follies. Try-outs weren't scheduled to start for another hour, yet the lobby was already packed. Tap shoes clackety-clacked and worn satin toe shoes, sticky with rosin, squeaked and spun over the marble floor. The smell of sweaty, leather jazz shoes mingled with noxious spurts of hairspray.

Faith was thrilled that all these people were auditioning. Many of them had come up to her in the past few days saying that they'd seen her production of *Alice in Wonderland* and really wanted to be in her segment of the show. It was only her second semester of freshman year, and she was already getting a good reputation as a director! And for the first time in her life, one of her productions was going to be staged in a real theater, with a real box office and real dressing rooms and a lighting board and hundreds of seats.

"Red leather, yellow leather. Red leather, yellow leather," a self-conscious voice articulated. Faith recognized Dante Borelli, a tall, wiry drama major from her dorm, standing just inside the door to the theater. Dressed in a T-shirt, loose black pants, and colorful suspenders, he breathed deeply in and out as he overexaggerated each syllable. "Red leather, yellow leather," he said more loudly when he noticed Faith.

Faith waved and moved on.

"Un bel di vedremo le varsi un fil di fumo . . ." A gorgeous soprano voice filled the lobby with sound, and Faith saw that it emanated from the

sturdy frame of her nextdoor neighbor Freya, an opera major who lived with Kimberly. Freya stopped singing when she saw Faith and pushed through the crowd toward her.

"I am very excited about this opportunity," Freya said in her German-accented voice. Freya's ruddy cheeks glowed against her pale, white skin, and her blond hair had been curled with a curling iron. "I would be so happy to sing before my fellow students."

"Of course I can't promise anything," Faith said, "but I'm sure you'll do great. And thank you so much for showing up today." Faith looked around for Kimberly. "Where's your roommate, Freya? I thought she was auditioning, too."

"She's right outside," Freya answered. "She had a little stomach ache, so she stepped out for some air."

"Is she all right?" Faith asked.

Freya nodded confidently. "It's nothing serious."

At that moment, Kimberly appeared in the doorway wearing a black leotard, black tights, and a wispy, black chiffon skirt. Her long, lean legs were well-muscled and her long arms looked graceful as she leaned against the doorjamb, looking around uncertainly.

"Over here!" Faith waved to her.

"Yoooo hooooo!" Freya sang.

At the unmistakable sound of her roommate's voice, Kimberly turned and started making her way through the singers and dancers.

"I'm so happy you came!" Faith squealed, giving Kimberly a hug. "How's your stomach?"

"I'm fine," Kimberly said, though her voice sounded tense.

"Maybe there's a bug going around," Faith suggested.

Kimberly smiled. "I'm sure that's it."

"Well, good luck," Faith said. She started to push her way toward the entrance to the auditorium. She felt totally uplifted by this huge turn-out. It almost made her forget the depressing news that Lauren wanted to move out. But maybe that would turn out okay, too. It still wasn't too late to get Lauren to change her mind.

"Faith!"

The anxious, breathy voice came from right behind her. Faith turned and saw Lauren looking around the lobby. She wore her green satin bomber jacket, black jeans, and a frightened expression.

"What are you doing here?" Faith asked in surprise. "Don't tell me you're planning to audition for my show?"

Lauren shook her head, and Faith noticed that there were dark circles under Lauren's violet eyes.

"Are you all right?" Faith asked, placing a comforting hand on her roommate's shoulder. "You look like you're going to be sick. You know, I think Kimberly has the same thing."

Lauren shook her head. "It's not physical," she said. "It's financial. Look, I know your auditions are going to start soon but do you have a minute? It's important."

"Sure," Faith said. "The audition doesn't start for another half hour. Why don't we sit here?"

Faith led Lauren to two folding chairs by the door. She had to push aside a huge shoulder bag filled with sheet music, audio cassettes, and pancake makeup to make room for their feet.

"Excuse me, that's mine!" said a girl with curly, red hair. She hefted the huge bag on her shoulder and gave Faith an indignant look.

"Sorry," Faith said. Then she turned back to Lauren.

"I am in serious trouble," Lauren said as she sat down. "Remember that notice I put up in the housing office about selling my dorm contract?"

"How could I forget?" Faith said glumly, leaning forward and placing her elbows on her knees.

Lauren nervously zipped and unzipped her jacket. "Maybe everyone's all set with their rooms," she said, "because no one has responded! No one's called, and no one's ripped off the little tabs I put on the bottom with my phone number on them."

Faith had to use every bit of dramatic skill she had to make herself look sad. What she really wanted to do was jump for joy! If Lauren couldn't sell her dorm contract, then Lauren would continue to be her roommate! Though Faith was genuinely sorry that Lauren had a problem, she couldn't help but feel glad for herself. "Maybe you need to give it more time," Faith said gently.

"I'm running out of time!" Lauren said, her voice uncharacteristically loud. "I've already put down the deposit on my room off campus. If I have to pay for both rooms, I'll go broke so fast they won't even let me finish the semester! What am I going to do?"

"Maybe your landlady at the new place will let you out of the lease," Faith said hopefully.

"Maybe I should just go up to people at random and tell them how great Coleridge Hall is. Maybe then someone will buy my dorm contract," Lauren joked with a grim face.

The girl with the red curls suddenly dropped

her heavy bag at Lauren's feet. "Honey!" she shouted in a brassy voice, "I am about to make your day!"

"Huh?" Lauren mumbled as the redhead unfolded another chair and plopped it down right between Lauren and Faith.

"Would you mind moving over a little?" the redhead asked Faith as she wriggled in the chair to get comfortable.

Up close, Faith could see that the girl's hair was not a natural shade of red. It was closer to orange, actually, bright orange, like dayglo paint. She seemed to be overflowing out of her lowcut, turquoise leotard and hot pink tights. Her face had been powdered pale, then brightened up with a heavy dose of blush, mascara, and red lipstick. Sparkling rhinestone bangles hung from her ears, and she wore a matching rhinestone bracelet. Her face wasn't conventionally pretty, but it was dazzlingly alive.

"Years from now," the redhead said to Lauren, "you'll tell your grandchildren that *I* was the one who came to your rescue and bought your dorm contract."

"Excuse me," Lauren said politely, "but I don't even know who you are."

"Not yet," the girl said. "But you will someday. Everybody will. Actually, you'll know a lot

sooner 'cause I'm about to tell you. My name's
Liza Ruff. I'm a freshman and a theater arts major. I've been *dying* to get into Coleridge, but I
didn't start here 'til second semester and all the
rooms were taken. Can you believe they put me
in an all-girls study dorm? *Me?* I wasn't made for
quiet. I was put on earth to *make noise!* And the
whole world's gonna hear me."

I think the whole world already can, Faith
thought as she inched her chair away from Liza.
Was this girl for real? Faith felt like she needed
sunglasses just to look at her.

"Are you serious?" Lauren asked, leaning eagerly toward Liza. "Would you really be interested in buying my dorm contract?"

"Interested?" Liza repeated. *"Interested?* If I
thought there was a chance I might get into
Coleridge, I'd crawl on my hands and knees to
get a dorm contract. I'd do anything! Actually, I
sort of stole that line from *Fiddler on the Roof.*
Did you ever see that play? It was great. Those
were Tzeitel's lines; she's the oldest daughter.
That part is perfect for me; Bette Midler played it
on Broadway."

Faith rolled her eyes at Lauren, but Lauren
gave her a "please-go-along-with-this" look. Was
Lauren really considering selling her contract to
this Bette Midler clone? Surely Lauren would act

more responsibly than that. She didn't even know this girl.

"How soon could you move in?" Lauren asked.

"Oh, right away," Liza said, squeezing Lauren's hand. "I can even pay you cash, if that will speed things up."

Things were going too fast already! *Slow down!* Faith wanted to tell Lauren. *Give it a chance! Your notice has only been up a couple of days. Someone else is bound to want it.*

". . . and this will be your new roommate, Faith Crowley," Lauren said excitedly, pointing to Faith. "She's really great, quiet, considerate, and she also happens to be directing this segment of the Follies."

Liza, who had virtually ignored Faith, now turned a thousand-watt grin on her. "Roomie!" she shouted, throwing her turquoise and rhinestone studded arms around her. "This is so exciting! Just think about it. We're going to be living together *and* working together on the Follies!"

Working together? The auditions hadn't even started yet. This girl was being pretty presumptuous. Now Faith sent Lauren a look that said "Say it isn't so!" How could Lauren do this to her? Lauren, her closest friend besides KC and Winnie. Lauren, who was so kind-hearted she'd trapped an ant that had been crawling in their room in order to bring it outside and set it free.

"Why don't you come by the room tonight?" Lauren said. "We'll sign the contract."

Lauren gave Faith a pleading look, mutely begging Faith's forgiveness, and Faith had no choice but to give it to her. While Faith's family certainly had nowhere near the money Lauren's had, Faith had never been broke, either. Who was to say what she might have done if she were in Lauren's place?

And maybe she was judging Liza too quickly. Sure, Liza was—well—colorful, but so was Winnie, and Winnie was one of her best friends! And Liza certainly seemed energetic and friendly. She was probably talented, too. Maybe that was why Liza felt so sure she'd be cast in the show.

Faith began to feel bad that she was being closed-minded. She was upset Lauren was leaving, but that was no reason not to give Liza a chance, especially if Liza was going to be her new roommate. And wouldn't it be great if Liza *did* get into the show? Then Faith would have a new friend to talk to about her work, someone else who'd understand how she felt.

Faith stood up. "It was very nice to meet you, Liza," she said cheerfully. "I'm sure you're going to give a wonderful audition. I'll see you inside."

Lauren gave Faith a grateful look, and Faith rushed off into the auditorium. The stage lights had already been turned on. Mikaela Harel, the music student who was going to be the accompanist, was warming up at the upright piano which had been wheeled onto the stage. Meredith, the junior in charge of the production, appeared from the wings in a rumpled blazer and wrinkled slacks.

"You ready?" he asked.

"Just about," Faith answered, unfastening her knapsack. She pulled out her clipboard with sheets of paper on which she'd neatly typed the names of each student auditioning. Boxes next to each name would indicate which number they might be right for. She'd also left blank space for comments.

"We've still got a few minutes," Faith said, "but with all those people out there, maybe we can start a little early."

Meredith shrugged. "Why not? Don't mind me, by the way. This is your segment. I'm just here to help out. You want me to call out the names in the lobby?"

"That would be great," Faith said, walking toward the stage to give Meredith a copy of her list. "Just call out three at a time and tell them to wait backstage."

Faith sat down on a worn, red velvet seat in the fourth row of the theater and propped her feet up between the seats in front of her. She flipped absentmindedly to the page with Liza's name and stared at it. Liza Ruff. A few minutes ago it was just another name on her list. Now it was her new roommate and, hopefully, her new friend. *I know I'm going to like her,* Faith told herself. The girl really did have charisma. She probably had a great singing voice, too. Her speaking voice was certainly loud and strong. The more Faith thought about it, the more sure she was that Liza would do a great job.

"A-hhhhem!" a loud voice was clearing itself loudly up on stage.

Faith looked up. Liza Ruff stood in the center of the stage, her fluorescent hair and rhinestones gleaming under the stage lights. Beneath the shiny turquoise leotard and hot pink tights, tightly hugging every overstuffed curve, was a pair of gold lame tap shoes. Liza looked completely relaxed on stage, and a little impatient.

Faith smiled up at her. "What are you going to sing?" she asked.

"What else?" Liza asked. "The number I'm going to do in the show. "When I Hear the Music" from *She's My Baby.*"

"Great!" Faith said, already getting used to

Liza's confidence. There was nothing wrong with having a positive attitude.

Mikaela began the rinkytink 1930s opening of the song. Liza positioned herself at the edge of the stage and opened her bright red lips to sing:

"When I hear the music, it does something to me,
The tingles shoot through me,
It feels like a new me . . ."

It was brutal. It was torture. In a word, Liza was awful. Faith sank into her seat and propped her clipboard in front of her face so Liza couldn't see her reaction. Liza sounded like a foghorn, very loud, and very off-key. Faith peeked over the top of her clipboard to see what Liza was doing now. Liza was strutting across the front of the stage, wiggling her generous turquoise hips and flirting with the invisible members of the audience. Then she did a little dance step that looked more like an elephant tripping over its own feet. Liza wasn't a performer. She was a bad joke.

Faith *wanted* to like her. Faith *wanted* to use her in the show. But there was no way she could. If she gave Liza a part, it would be worse than showing favoritism to a roommate. It would be theatrical suicide!

Eight

*O*K, *what do I feel strongly about? Hmmmm. Let's see—the price of imported leather goods, like Italian shoes, is way too high, so that the average person can't afford them, which means all Americans can't afford to dress well, which is really undemocratic. No, that makes me sound too superficial, and anyway nobody else is going to think that's an important issue.*

KC, dressed in a baggy U. of S. sweatshirt over black leggings and mismatched socks, sat at her desk Wednesday evening, chewing on a pencil. She still had a few minutes before Sheldon Copperstein came over and she was trying desperately to come up with at least one topic so he wouldn't think she was a total lamebrain. So far, though, nothing was coming to mind.

KC sighed and put her feet up on her desk. Maybe she should just wait for Sheldon. After all, she was paying him ten bucks an hour to help her. She'd been supposed to go over to his room tonight, but he'd called a few minutes ago and asked if he could come to her room instead. He'd been remounting some stamps and didn't want anything to get messed up.

KC had to laugh at this. Did Sheldon think she was going to turn on a blow dryer and blow his stamps out of the albums? The guy had obviously been holed up in his room too long. KC embellished the mental picture she already had of him. Not only was he skinny and pimply, but he had to be really pale, too, from all those hours spent indoors, huddled over his stamp collection. Maybe he didn't even go out for meals. Maybe he just collected graham crackers in the dining commons and lived on that. And he probably never opened his window for fear a breeze would come in and blow away his stamps.

KC checked her watch. It was five minutes to seven. She briefly considered changing into something less grungy, but then didn't bother. After all, Sheldon wasn't someone she wanted to impress.

Knock! Knock!

Sheldon was early. KC swung her legs off the desk and padded across the bare floor to the door. *Now remember,* she told herself, *he's here to help you, so be nice. Don't look down on him just because he's a nerd.*

KC turned the knob and opened the door.

"Hi," said the guy in the hallway. "I'm Sheldon."

KC was speechless.

Standing at least six feet tall, with wide shoulders and muscular arms, Sheldon, the stamp collector, was anything but a nerd. Actually, the right word to describe him was *built—and* gorgeous. There wasn't a pimple within ten miles of him. He had clear, bronzed skin and thick, dark, wavy hair. His eyes were a pale shade of green, deepset over high cheekbones.

The guy had style, too. He was wearing an olive green shirt that brought out the green of his eyes. Through the waistband of his black pants was a black, snakeskin belt with a silver Western buckle. His loafers were also made of black snakeskin, and he had a letter jacket tucked under one arm.

KC wanted to slam the door and change her clothes, but it was too late. Sheldon had already seen her in her slob outfit. There was only one thing she could do.

"Won't you come in?" KC asked politely.

Sheldon hesitated for a moment. "I think we'd better verify that I'm in the right place," he said. "I wouldn't want to start tutoring you and then discover that you're not KC Angeletti."

KC laughed. "That's funny!" she said.

Sheldon stared at her expressionlessly. "It wasn't a joke."

KC shrugged. "Who else would I be?" she asked. "You're definitely in the right place."

"Excuse me," came a twangy, irritated voice from down the hall. "Would you guys mind keeping it down? We do have a twenty-four-hour quiet rule here in Langston House, and you're disturbing the peace!"

KC poked her head outside her doorway and saw Marielle Danner heading toward them. Marielle looked chic, as usual. She wore a royal blue wool suit, and her heavy gold charm bracelet jangled as she sauntered down the hall. After being banished from Tri Beta, she had ended up in Langston. KC knew Marielle blamed her for what had happened, but she tried her best to be polite.

"Hello, Marielle," KC said.

Marielle paused for a moment and gave Sheldon an appraising, approving look. Her charm bracelet clinked as she ran a manicured hand through her chin-length brown hair. Then, without another word, she continued down the hall without returning KC's greeting.

"Come in, Sheldon," KC said, placing a hand on his thick, well-muscled upper arm. The material of his shirt felt soft. "Please sit down."

Sheldon slung his letter jacket over the back of one of the chairs in front of KC's desk and sat down. "Well?" he asked, fixing his pale green eyes on her.

"Uh . . . right," KC said, as she sat down in the other chair. "Well, I'm having trouble writing a persuasive essay for English class. I can't focus on a topic, let alone organize my thoughts, and the guy at the Learning Center said you could help. I really need to do well on this. If I don't bring up my English grade, I won't be able to stay in my sorority. Maybe that sounds silly to you, but . . ."

"No," Sheldon interrupted her. "I understand. But let's not go off on a tangent. Let's just get right in and attack the immediate problem. You say you can pick any topic for this essay?"

KC nodded. "I almost wish they'd given us something specific. With the whole world to choose from, I don't know where to start."

"Start with *you,*" Sheldon said forcefully. "The topic has to be something that's important to you, or you won't know enough or care enough about it to be persuasive. What kinds of things are you interested in?"

"Well, money, to be honest," KC said. "I'd like to be an Economics major, and my business course is really the only one I'm doing well in."

"Okay, let's start there," Sheldon said. "The economy's a big issue right now."

"That's right," KC said. "Stores are closing all over the country. Big companies are laying off thousands of people. Economists say we're in a recession."

"Are we?" Sheldon asked. "I've heard some parts of the country are doing better than others."

"*I* think we are," KC said. "I don't know how long it will last, but I think the country's in trouble."

"There's your topic," Sheldon said. "Make your argument that the country's heading into a recession. Now we've just got to figure out what your reasons are, then organize them."

As Sheldon plucked a pen from several clipped to the breast pocket of his shirt, KC found herself staring at him. He was a definite hunk. And if he looked this good in regular clothes, KC couldn't help wondering how great he'd look all dressed up, as her escort to the Gamma dance. If KC walked in with Sheldon on her arm, she'd get nothing but admiring, envious glances from her Tri Beta sisters. They'd probably drool all over their party dresses.

And Sheldon had more than looks. He was also smart, a jock, and a great dresser. A guy with credentials like these didn't come along every day. KC knew all she probably had to do was gaze meaningfully into his eyes and ask him about his stamp collection for him to show interest in her. In no time he would be asking her out. Then she'd invite him to the Gamma dance and . . .

KC turned toward Sheldon. He raised his eyes to meet hers. *So, Sheldon, tell me about your stamp collection* . . . She could hear the words in her head, but for some reason she couldn't speak them out loud. She didn't want to ask Sheldon anything except, how to write a better essay.

KC knew that the reason holding her back was Peter. So what if he didn't make as good an impression on her sorority sisters. She cared so much about him that there wasn't any room left for her to care about anyone else, no matter how good-looking. She'd learned her lesson after dumping Peter for gorgeous Warren Manning at the Winter Formal.

"KC?" Sheldon said. "If we're to make progress, I require your full attention."

"Hmmm?" KC looked once again into Sheldon's handsome face and realized he'd been sitting with his pen poised over her notebook for several minutes. "I'm sorry," she said. "Where were we?"

At the end of an hour, KC had a rough outline for her essay, with each of the points neatly labeled by Sheldon.

"Now you should be able to start writing," Sheldon said. "And by the way, my fee is ten dollars."

KC pulled her wallet out of her purse and handed Sheldon the money. "It was worth it," she said. "But how will I know if my essay's good after I write it?" KC asked. "I mean, I know all the rules of grammar, and everything, but how will I know if it's persuasive?"

"I could come back for another session after you've written it," he said. "We can go over it and fine-tune it. When's it due?"

"Friday."

"Hmmm . . . then we'll have to meet tomorrow. Do you think you can have it written by then?"

KC nodded.

Sheldon pulled a leather organizer out of his jacket pocket and flipped it open on KC's desk. "Let's see," he said, scanning his Thursday appointments, written in tiny, precise handwriting. "Yes, I believe I could squeeze you in at four P.M. But I only have an hour."

"Pencil me in," KC said, watching as Sheldon filled in her name and room number between all his other dates. "Gee," she remarked. "You must have an active social life."

Sheldon looked surprised. "Oh no," he said. "I'm far too busy to socialize. Between debating, my stamp and coin collections, and varsity soccer, I have very little time to meet people."

"That's too bad," KC said. "I'm sure there are plenty of girls on campus who would love to meet you."

Sheldon shrugged. "Then they've exercised amazing self-restraint," he said. "I've never been approached."

"Maybe they're waiting for you to approach them," KC suggested. "Most girls are pretty shy about that sort of thing."

Sheldon sighed. "I'm glad that excuse works for girls," he said. "What makes people think it's any easier for guys to walk up to someone?"

"I never really thought about that," KC said.

"I guess it's easier when someone else does the introducing for you." Then she sat up straight in her chair. "Sheldon," she said, "I have a great idea. Would you like to meet a friend of mine? She's pretty, blond, a freshman, and a wonderful person. I think you'd really like her."

Sheldon stood up to put on his purple and gold jacket. "What's her name?"

"Faith Crowley. I've known her forever. She's a Theater Arts major, and she's really talented."

"A thespian," Sheldon mused. "Interesting. Does she like stamps?"

"There's only one way to find out," KC said. "Why don't you meet her and ask her yourself?"

Sheldon shrugged. "Why not?"

"Great!" KC exclaimed. "I'll set the whole thing up, and give you the details when I see you tomorrow."

Nine

"**Y**ou look like you're dressed for Halloween, Winnie!" Faith exclaimed later that night as she opened the door to her room. Winnie, standing in the hallway, wore pink bicycle shorts over shiny purple tights and an orange T-shirt that said "I'm Still Waiting for the Great Pumpkin." She held a large shopping bag in each hand and paper streamers were strung around her neck like an Hawaiian lei.

"Yeah," KC called from where she lounged on Faith's bed, "a trick-or-treater who just got back from vacation. What's with the paper necklace?"

"They're decorations!" Winnie said, grinning, as she entered Faith's room. She dumped the heavy bags on the floor and removed the purple and yellow streamers from around her neck. "I thought we should celebrate the casting of your show, and I found these hanging in the basement of my dorm. One of the jocks had a birthday party."

After agonizing all day, Faith had finally posted the cast list that evening at the University Theater. It wasn't that selecting the performers had been difficult; there were enough talented people to choose from. The agony had come from the one person she *hadn't* chosen. Faith hadn't seen Liza since the cast list went up, and she wasn't looking forward to it. Liza had been so sure she'd get to sing "When I Hear the Music." At the very least, she'd be disappointed, but Faith had a sinking feeling that bold, brassy, larger-than-life Liza was going to react a lot more strongly than that. And with Liza moving in, there'd be nowhere Faith could escape to to get away from her new roommate's rage.

"Do you have any Scotch tape?" Winnie asked. "I'll put up the streamers."

Faith opened her desk drawer and got a roll of tape. "Here," she said, handing it to Winnie. "I'll start unpacking the rest of the stuff."

Winnie pulled Faith's desk chair to the door,

climbed on, and taped up one end of the streamers near the ceiling.

"I'll help you," KC said, jumping up off the bed. She took the Scotch tape from Winnie and tore off several strips which she stuck on the back of her hand.

"Wow!" Faith said, lifting Winnie's popcorn maker out of one bag. The other bag held several bottles of soda, a bag of nacho cheese Doritos, and a box of Hostess chocolate cupcakes. "You're really serious about this!"

"We have serious reasons to celebrate!" Winnie said, hopping down off the chair and dragging it to the center of the room. KC followed and continued handing Winnie strips of tape. "Things are going great for all of us. You cast your show, KC got into Tri Beta, and Josh and I are at least trying to talk. Maybe one day we'll actually get more than five minutes together without an interruption."

Faith knelt on the floor to plug in the popcorn popper. "I wish I could celebrate the fact that Lauren wasn't leaving," she said glumly, "but Lauren sold her dorm contract to Liza a little while ago, so I guess it's official." Faith sat down where she was and leaned back against the wall with a sigh.

"Is that where Lauren is, signing the contract?" Winnie asked, taping the streamers to the light fixture at the center of the ceiling. "I wanted her to come to our party."

"No." Faith pulled her knees up to her chest and hugged them. "After she signed the papers, she went with Dash to an open lecture for his master journalism class. I guess she's so busy with Dash and the paper and her job that I wouldn't really have spent much time with her even if she *did* still live here." Faith sighed again and rested her head on her knees.

Winnie hopped off her chair, leaving the purple and yellow streamers hanging straight down from the middle of the room, and knelt down beside Faith. "Don't be bummed, Faith," she said, sitting beside her on the floor. "You'll still see her."

KC opened the bag of Doritos and brought it over. "And you've still got us," she said, sitting down on Faith's other side.

Faith reached into the Dorito bag and pulled out a handful of chips. Then she looked from KC to Winnie and smiled at their concerned, familiar faces. "You guys are so great!" she said. "I'm lucky to have friends like you. And aside from Lauren, I guess there's no real reason for me to be glum. I got some really good people for my segment," she told her friends. "We're already set up to start rehearsing tomorrow."

Winnie hopped up and dragged the chair to the far end of the room. "Who's going to be in it?" she asked as she climbed on the chair and taped the streamers to the wall over Faith's bed.

Faith stood up and poured a cupful of popcorn into the popcorn maker. "Well, I cast Dante Borelli for the patter-song, "Trouble in River City" from *The Music Man*. He's got great diction. And guess who I picked for the song and dance solo?"

There was a knock on the door.

"To be continued," Faith said, as she turned on the popcorn maker and went to open the door.

Kimberly stood in the hallway, wearing a blue, crushed velvet, cat suit that hugged her tall, lean frame. Her feet were bare, and large, gold, hoop earrings swung from her ears. "Faith, can I talk . . ." Kimberly paused when KC appeared behind Faith in the doorway. "Oh, hi, you guys," she said. "Did I interrupt anything?"

"No way!" Faith said, dragging Kimberly into the room. "We're having a party, and you have just as much reason to celebrate as we do. KC, Winnie, I'd like to present to you one of the stars of my production, Miss Kimberly Dayton. Kimberly will be performing the solo song and dance number "When I Hear the Music" at the U. of S. Follies."

"Yay!" Winnie shouted, clapping from up on her chair.

KC, too, clapped, then offered Kimberly some Doritos. "Congratulations!" she said, as Faith sat Kimberly down on Lauren's bed.

"What does everybody want to drink?" Faith asked, pulling some paper cups out of Winnie's shopping bag. On her desk, behind the yellow plastic of the popcorn popper, hard, little kernels exploded into fluffy clouds of popcorn.

"Whatever you're having," Kimberly said. "Say, where's Lauren? Did she go through with the dirty deed?"

Faith sighed as she poured out sodas for KC and Winnie.

"Well, that answers my question," Kimberly said. "I'm really sorry, Faith. But at least you'll have me right next door." She sat on the floor, leaning against Faith's desk, and extended her long legs.

"I know," Faith said, pouring herself a Seven-Up and sitting next to Kimberly. "And I'm really happy about that."

When everyone had settled on the floor with their soda and a huge bowl of popcorn, Faith found herself thinking about Lauren again. So now it was final, signed and sealed. Lauren was really moving out.

"Hey!" Winnie said, breaking into Faith's thoughts. "I thought we were celebrating! You've been nibbling on that same piece of popcorn for the past five minutes."

Faith looked up at Winnie and tried to smile. "Sorry," she said. "I can't stop thinking about Lauren. It's so confusing being happy and sad at the same time. I feel like I'm on a see-saw. First I think about the show and I'm up. Then I think about Lauren . . ." Faith trailed off and nibbled thoughtfully on her piece of popcorn.

"I think you need something to tip the balance," KC said. "In fact, I think it's time I told you the reason I came over tonight."

"You mean you had an ulterior motive?" Faith asked, pretending to be hurt. "I thought you just came over because you wanted to spend time with me."

"Of course I did!" KC said. "But I have really good news for you that I wanted to deliver in person."

"What?" Faith asked, finally popping the piece of popcorn in her mouth. "Did you figure out a way to bankroll Lauren's education so she can buy back her dorm contract?"

"Thanks for your faith in me, Faith, but even *I*

am not as great a financial wizard as that. If I were, I wouldn't be broke all the time."

"So what is it?" Winnie asked, crawling along the floor toward KC and cupping her hand to her ear. "I love good news!"

"Faith," KC asked, "what is the one area of your life that is currently on hold?"

"That's easy," Faith said. "My love life. But then again, a love life can't be on hold unless you have one, which I certainly don't."

"That's all about to change," KC announced triumphantly. "I am going to introduce you to the most incredibly good-looking, intelligent hunk you have ever met in your life. You're going to thank me, Faith, believe me."

Faith perked up slightly. If KC thought a guy was gorgeous, then he probably looked like a professional model. "What's his name?" Faith asked.

"Sheldon Copperstein."

Faith couldn't help laughing. "I hate to say it," she said, "but that doesn't sound like the name of a hunk."

KC nodded seriously. "I know," she said. "I thought the same thing. But when he appeared on my doorstep to tutor me, I realized how wrong I had been. He's tall, muscular, with dark hair and green eyes, and he plays varsity soccer."

"Another soccer player," Faith mused. Her ex-boyfriend, Brooks Baldwin, played intramural soccer. "Maybe it's fate."

"And he's not an empty mannequin like Warren Manning," KC added. "This guy is brilliant. He's even on the debating team."

"If you don't want him, *I'll* take him," Kimberly said to Faith. "Go for it."

"Sounds great," Faith said. "When do I meet him?"

"How about Saturday afternoon?" KC said. "I know you have rehearsal, but maybe we can squeeze it in right before."

"I guess I could spare a half hour," Faith said.

"Great! I'm seeing Sheldon tomorrow to go over my English paper, so I'll check with him and get back to you. By the way, have I mentioned how good-looking he is?"

"Now you're scaring me!" Faith said. "If he's that gorgeous, he probably won't even want to talk to a simple earthling like me."

"He'll talk to you," KC said. "Just ask him about his stamp collection."

"His *what?*" Faith started to ask, but Winnie was raising her paper cup.

"Excuse me," Winnie said, "but I think it's time we got down to the real business of this party. I'd like to propose a toast to my old pal and soon to be famous director, Ms. Faith Crowley, for casting what I'm sure will be the most noteworthy segment of this year's Follies."

"Here, here," KC said, raising her paper cup.

Faith and Kimberly raised their cups, too.

"And *I'd* like to toast one of my stars who gave a splendid audition today and who will, I'm sure, sing and dance her way into the hearts of U. of S.-ers when she performs in two weeks."

"Kim-ber-ly! Kim-ber-ly!" Winnie chanted.

Kimberly looked down, embarrassed. "It's a little premature to celebrate, don't you think? Wait until after the performance before you congratulate me. You may not even want to . . ."

"No false modesty in my room," Faith said. "You'll be great and you know it."

"Speaking of great," Kimberly said, "we should really get Freya in here, too. She's so happy that you cast her for the love duet."

"Dante . . . Freya . . . Kimberly . . . sounds like it's going to be a Coleridge Hall spectacular," KC said to Faith. "You've cast all your neighbors. I don't suppose there was any nepotism involved."

"I know how it sounds," Faith admitted, "but I honestly thought the people I chose were the best. Coleridge Hall is the creative arts dorm, after all."

"I didn't think of that," KC said. "Sorry."

"Of course, I'm not denying that I wanted to work with my friends," Faith added, putting her arm around Kimberly, "but I'm lucky that my friends happen to be so talented!"

"What about your new roommate?" Winnie asked. "Didn't she try out?"

"Yes," Faith answered, a small knot starting to form in her stomach. She had almost forgotten about Liza.

"And what happened?" Winnie asked.

There was a shattering sound as the door to Faith's room flew open. Faith cringed as a large, battered aluminum trunk shot through the doorway, skidded along the floor, and overturned the paper cups of soda. The trunk was covered with stickers of rainbows, bright red lips, smiley faces, logos for Broadway shows, and flags of foreign countries.

A chilling breeze followed the trunk, and all heads turned to the doorway. There, legs planted wide, fists buried in her substantial hips, stood Liza Ruff. Her outfit was comical—purple sneakers, red and white striped tights, black puffy skirt, and a bustier top. Her curly, orange hair was wilder than ever. But there was nothing funny about the expression on her face. Her blue eyes flashed. Her lips, with the red lipstick partially gone, were drawn into a scowl as she looked down at the party on the floor.

Nervously, Faith stood up to greet her new roommate. "Hi!" she said. "I'm sorry about all this stuff. I wasn't expecting you so soon."

Liza focused her angry gaze on Winnie. "You look like a normal person," Liza said. "Tell your friend Faith that as of this moment, I am not speaking to her."

"Why not?" Winnie asked. "You haven't even moved in yet!"

"*She* knows why not," Liza said with a sniff. "And you just made the biggest mistake of your directing career," she said to Faith, forgetting she wasn't speaking to her. "You've overlooked one of the greatest performing talents ever to travel west of the Hudson River. I should have known better than to leave New York to come out here to school. But you'll be sorry. When Joan Rivers interviews me on her talk show, I'm going to mention you specifically by name as the director who refused to give me a part. Now I'm going to get the rest of my stuff." Giving the trunk one last kick with her purple sneaker, Liza turned around and stomped out of the room.

"I guess you didn't put her in your show,"

Winnie observed, grabbing a handful of popcorn and popping it into her mouth.

Faith shook her head. The celebration had just come to an abrupt end.

Ten

"It's Dave Baker, the human battering-ram!" Eric Bitterman shouted as he tightened his grip around Dave's shoulders.

Steve Powell, who held up Dave's feet, lifted them so they were even with Dave's head. "You ready to go, Dave?" he asked companionably.

"Ready!" Dave said in his hoarse, raspy voice, tucking his chin in to his chest and pressing his thick arms tight against his sides.

Josh Gaffey hadn't staked out a chair in the lobby of Forest Hall to watch the jocks perform their side show. The reason he'd spent the past hour sitting by the front door was that he was hoping Winnie might walk through it. After several weeks of practically living in the Computer Center, Josh had finally finished his research paper. It now sat neatly typed on his desk, ready to be delivered to his professor first thing in the morning. And now that he had some free time, he wanted to spend it with Winnie so they could figure out what was going on between them.

"One, two, three . . . CHARGE!" Eric yelled as he and Steve started to run, carrying Dave, toward a group of girls who stood talking in the lobby of Forest Hall.

One of the girls, a chunky, blond field hockey player named Mary Ellen, screamed "Watch out!" as she and her friends scattered in all directions. Mary Ellen headed straight for Josh's feet, which were stuck out in front of him. At the same moment she tried to jump over his legs, Josh tried to pull them in out of the way, causing her to trip and go sprawling across the beige linoleum, right into a keg of beer. The keg toppled over, spilling the amber, sudsy liquid all over the floor. A damp, yeasty smell filled the air.

"Bitterman!" Mary Ellen screamed, clambering to her feet. "I'm gonna get you for this!" Skating through the beer, she raced down the hall after Eric, Steve, and Dave.

What was keeping Winnie? Josh had stopped

by her room, and Melissa had said Winnie was over in Coleridge Hall, visiting her friend Faith, so Josh had planted himself in the lobby to wait. But it had been nearly an hour. Josh wished she'd come home. After weeks of waiting, he felt like he couldn't wait one more minute.

"Eeeeeee!" Mary Ellen screamed as she slid through the beer, back into the lobby, on her rear end. A tall, gangly girl from the track team slid right behind her, followed by a muscular swimmer with a long, brown braid.

"That was fun!" Mary Ellen said to the other girls, as they landed in a pile near Josh. "Only don't tell Eric. I'm still mad at him about the Jell-O they poured into the toilets in our bathroom. That was so disgusting!"

"I know," agreed the tall girl. "I looked down and saw all this shiny, green stuff. I didn't know *what* was in there. We really have to get them back for that."

"Especially before they pull their next stunt," the girl with the braid said. "From what my spies tell me, they've got something cooking."

"What?" asked the other two, together.

"I don't know any specifics," replied the girl with the braid. "All I heard was that they're calling it 'The Big Switcheroo.' But whatever it is, we can do something even worse. Maybe we could sneak into their rooms and throw all their clothes out the window!"

Josh shook his head as he listened to the girls on the floor. The girl jocks were just as bad as the guy jocks! Sometimes Josh wondered what had possessed him to live in Forest Hall. The only sport he took seriously was Frisbee. But at least he could say one thing about his dorm—you never knew what to expect. That kept things interesting. Sort of like Winnie.

Josh looked up again at the front door, but she still hadn't appeared. He tried to send Winnie a message telepathically. *Winnie, come home!* Then Josh laughed at himself. He was acting just as crazy as Winnie. But he couldn't help himself. Now that his head was clear of all the data and statistics that had been floating through it the past few weeks, all he could think about was Winnie. No, it was more than just thinking. It was a physical ache, a need to see her, be with her, talk to her—and to find out if she had been the person who took his call at the Crisis Hotline.

Just thinking about it made his face feel hot. She couldn't have been on the other end of the line. The odds of that happening had to be one in . . . How many people worked at that hotline anyway? And how many women? The person he'd spoken to had definitely been female. If he knew the numbers, he could work out the probability on his computer.

But that was silly. All he had to do was look at the evidence. Okay, so he'd spoken to a woman, but it hadn't sounded like Winnie. Of course, whoever she was hadn't said much, so he couldn't be sure.

If Winnie had answered his call, though, she knew how he still felt about her. That might even be why she had come up to him and kissed him out of the blue not too long ago. The kiss probably meant she also still cared, but it also meant that he'd blown his cover. So much for passing himself off as the cool, level-headed one in the relationship. If Winnie had been the one he'd talked to, she'd know, now, that she wasn't the only one who'd nearly gone over the edge. Josh had teetered on the brink himself, and it was only the *hope* that Winnie still cared that kept him from losing his balance completely.

"Mary Ellen Gluck, you get back here!" shouted Eric Bitterman as Mary Ellen ran through the lobby, waving a pair of boxer shorts above her head like a flag. The shorts were white with red hearts.

"Try and catch me!" Mary Ellen shouted as she skidded on the puddle of beer, slipped, regained her balance, and careened into the front door, just as Winnie pushed it open from the outside.

Mary Ellen bounced off the front door into Eric's arms, who proceeded to throw her over his shoulder and carry her, kicking and screaming, down the hall. Josh could barely resist the urge to do the same to Winnie. All he wanted was to wrap his arms around her and cover her face with kisses and take her upstairs to his room where they could finally be alone.

"Hi!" Winnie said, smiling.

Josh just looked at her and smiled back. If he could feel this good just looking at her, he'd spend the rest of his life in the lobby, waiting for her to come through the door.

"Are you on your way in or out?" Winnie asked wistfully, hugging the popcorn popper tightly to her chest.

"Neither," Josh said. "I finally finished my research paper, so I was just . . . uh . . . hanging out."

Winnie's eyes brightened, and she wiggled her eyebrows. "Do you mean to tell me that you're ready to rejoin the human race?"

"Actually, there's one particular representative of the species that I would most like to spend time with," Josh said, taking a step closer and staring down at her sparkling, brown eyes.

Winnie grinned up at him. "Allow me to introduce myself," she said. "Winnifred S. Gottlieb, ambassador-at-large. I've been appointed by a world commission to ease your transition back into society."

"Why, thank you," Josh said, offering Winnie his arm. "Would you care to accompany me to my room, ambassador?"

Winnie slipped her arm through his, and the touch of her fingers sent a warmth flooding through his body. "Is your roommate going to be there?" she asked as they climbed the stairs to the second floor. Their feet trudged in sync, echoing against the walls.

"Believe it or not," Josh said, "Mikoto's researching a poli-sci paper at the library, so he won't be back for a couple of hours."

"Oh really?" Winnie asked, looking up at him with a sexy smile. "So we'll be able to . . . talk . . . without being interrupted?"

Josh covered Winnie's hand with his own. "Nothing in the world will come between us," Josh said. "Not roommates, not jocks, and not my research paper."

As they emerged from the stairwell, Josh wrapped his arm around Winnie's firm waist and pulled her closer. He nuzzled her hair as they walked down the hall and paused outside his room. Without letting go of Winnie, Josh unlocked the door with his other hand.

"Nothing will get in our way this time," Josh said, gazing tenderly at Winnie as the door slid open. "See?"

Winnie wasn't looking at him. She was looking straight ahead, through the doorway, with her mouth wide open. "Uh oh . . ." she said.

"What's wrong?" Josh asked, turning to see what Winnie was looking at.

The room looked perfectly ordinary. It had two beds, two desks, two chairs, and two dressers. The white, lace curtains were pulled back with satin ribbons, and posters of movie stars Mel Gibson and Alec Brady covered the walls. Stuffed animals covered one bed, and the other had a pink bedspread. It was a perfectly ordinary room. But it wasn't his.

Josh stepped back to look at the number on the door. 141. That was his room number. Were they on the wrong floor or in the wrong building? Or was he going crazy?

"Josh?" Winnie asked in confusion. "Do you have a new roommate, or is there something you haven't told me?"

"I think there's something someone hasn't told *me,*" Josh said, entering the room.

Winnie followed him. "Hey!" she said, pointing to a "Computer Nerds do it Better" sticker on the window. "I recognize that. You put that up there. This is definitely your room."

"Then where's all my stuff?" Josh asked.

"It's got to be a practical joke," Winnie said. "I heard the jocks were planning something really big."

"The Big Switcheroo . . ." Josh said softly, remembering what he'd overheard in the lobby. "This must have been what they meant. They switch all the stuff in your room with someone else's. Very funny."

Winnie put her popcorn popper on the bare desk, then sat on the bed with the stuffed animals. "At least it's cozy. And these curtains are nicer than yours."

Pushing aside a purple elephant and a green dragon, Josh sat next to Winnie on the bed. "Well, I guess we can still . . . talk, even if it does feel like someone else's room."

"What shall we talk about?" she asked softly, running her finger along the back of his neck.

"Hmmm . . ." Josh tried to remember what it had been that seemed so important, but his mind didn't seem to be working. All he felt were Winnie's caressing fingers and the growing warmth inside him. "Come here," he said, scooping up her legs and pulling them over his lap. Her legs were bare and smooth.

"You'd better not do that," Winnie warned as Josh ran his hand up and down her leg, "or I might lose control."

"Oh yeah?" Josh challenged, pulling her even closer. Her body felt so good pressed against his, and her eyes were so full of love, exactly like they had been before her old boyfriend, Travis, had come to town. But now it seemed as if Travis had never existed.

Without letting go of Winnie, Josh lay her on the bed and let his lips brush softly over her cheeks, over her eyes, her nose, and finally, over her full lips, which parted in response. She fit so perfectly into his arms and his life. When she was with him, he could forget about everything else —exams, deadlines, papers. . . .

"Aaagh!" Josh shouted suddenly, feeling like he'd just been thrown in a vat of icy water. He jerked away from Winnie and leaped off the bed.

"What's the matter?" Winnie asked in alarm.

"My research paper!" Josh shouted, rushing toward the empty desk by the window. "I didn't even think about that when they switched the room around. My research paper was sitting on my desk, and now it's gone!"

"Oh no!" Winnie cried. She jumped up, scattering the stuffed animals all over the bed and floor.

"You don't think they would have thrown it out, do you?" Josh asked as he frantically began to search through the books and papers on the other desk. "I can't believe this. After all the work I did, if those dumb jocks lost it, I'll kill them. I'll bash them over the head with my computer, I'll . . ."

"Calm down," Winnie yelled. "It's probably sitting on someone else's desk right now."

"But whose?" Josh asked. "Whose stuff is this?"

"It's definitely someone in this dorm," Winnie said, "and obviously two girls. We'll just bang on every door in Forest Hall until we find your paper. Don't worry. It's got to be here somewhere."

As Winnie rushed out the door ahead of him, Josh paused for a moment to look back at the bed where they'd just been sitting. It had felt so good to be together. He still didn't know whether Winnie had answered his call to the Crisis Hotline or not and he still didn't know where their relationship was heading. All he knew was that it had felt good to be together again. But there wasn't time to think about that now. He had to find his paper. The moment had been lost again.

Eleven

Even in black and white, frozen and two-dimensional, she seemed to live and breathe. KC's large, gray eyes sparkled playfully, then flashed defiantly, then shone with tender concern as Peter ran his magnifier down the proof sheet from their photo session two days before.

Peter wasn't too modest to admit he was a talented photographer, but something incredible had happened during the shoot with KC. Maybe it was the chemistry between them, maybe it was her bone structure, maybe it was just luck, but he'd never ended up with so many great photographs. These were good enough to put on a magazine cover. He didn't know how he was going to choose just six for his project.

KC would definitely have an opinion. He wanted to show them to her anyway. It was the perfect excuse to stop by her room, not that he really needed an excuse anymore. He'd been a lot more confident about her feelings for him ever since she'd invited him to the Gamma dance—and kissed him with so much passion.

Carefully placing the proof sheets between two pieces of cardboard, Peter slipped the whole thing into an envelope, then tucked the envelope into his black, canvas bag. Grabbing his denim jacket from where it hung over his desk chair, he slung the bag over his shoulder and headed out the door for Langston House. He briefly considered calling KC's room first, to make sure she was there, but decided against it. He wanted to surprise her.

Whistling to himself, Peter took off across the green toward a cluster of large old houses. Originally, they'd been the U. of S. administration buildings. Now they were the single-sex study dorms. KC's dorm, Langston House, was right in the middle, with lace curtains and a covered porch.

Peter practically flew up the steps of Langston House. It wasn't simply that he was eager to show KC the pictures. Six hours in the darkroom staring at her image had made him even more eager to prove to himself that she was real— warm flesh and blood that he could take in his arms. More than anything, he wanted to kiss her again, secure in the knowledge that she wanted to kiss him back.

He was even looking forward to the Gamma dance despite the fact that it would be full of frat brats and sorority snobs. Though he hadn't told KC yet, Peter was planning to blow a lot of money renting a designer tuxedo for the occasion. He knew the tux wouldn't turn him into a stud, but at least if he were dressed properly, KC wouldn't feel embarrassed to be seen with him.

No, wait. He had to give himself more credit than that. This time he was certain. KC really liked him. This time it was finally safe to let his guard down and show her how much he liked her back.

Peter's sneakered feet bounced down the quiet, carpeted hallway. He paused in front of KC's door and knocked loudly.

Marielle slowed her pace as she walked down the second floor of Langston Hall. The guy knocking on KC's door looked familiar. Was it because she'd seen him before or because he looked like a lot of other guys? Then Marielle suddenly re-membered that he was the photographer who'd taken pictures for the Classic Calendar last semes-ter. His name was Peter something and she'd seen him more than once on campus and in the dorm with KC.

Suddenly Marielle smiled. She was starting to get an idea. It was KC's fault that she was stuck here in the dorms, banished forever from the Tri Betas. And now it was time to pay KC back, once and for all.

"May I help you?" Marielle asked sweetly as she approached Peter. "Are you looking for someone?"

"Yes," Peter said. "I'm looking for KC Angeletti."

Marielle pretended to think for a minute. "Let's see," she said, touching a red, manicured fingernail to her chin. "KC was here just a min-ute ago. Now where did she go? Oh yes, that's right. She left here with this incredibly hunky guy. I think they were going over to his dorm room."

"Excuse me?" Peter asked, his mouth hanging open, his face pale. Marielle knew her poisoned dart had hit the bullseye.

"Oh, I'm sorry," Marielle said. "I guess that wasn't enough of a description, not that there are many guys on campus as gorgeous as he is. I believe this fellow was six-feet-two or so, really muscular, almost like a professional bodybuilder, no, more like a model, I'd say. He had dark, wavy hair, green eyes, and he was wearing a letter jacket."

Peter's shoulders slumped and his eyes clouded over.

"It's not the first time I've seen them alone together," Marielle said. "The hunk . . . I mean, the guy was over here just the other night."

"I see," Peter said. His face seemed to have hardened, and a tiny muscle twitched in his cheek. "Of course, we can't jump to any conclusions," he muttered, almost to himself.

"Excuse me?" Marielle asked, arranging her face into an expression of tender concern.

"Nothing," Peter said, managing a grim smile. "Thanks for your help."

Squeak! Squeak! Squeak!

Faith couldn't stand the horrible, grating sound of the dolly's wheels against the hall floor. The closer they got, the closer they were to taking Lauren and her possessions away forever. Faith squeezed her eyes shut and tried to focus on the sound of Freya's voice next door, practicing scales, her rich soprano filling the corridors of Coleridge Hall. But she couldn't blot it out. Lauren was really leaving.

Even after Lauren had signed her dorm contract over to Liza last night, Faith had still held on to the hope that somehow, something would happen to keep Lauren on campus. But the only thing that happened was that Lauren had appeared in the room this afternoon with half a dozen brown cardboard boxes. Faith had to face the truth.

She opened her eyes and surveyed the chaos that was her room. Boxes covered the floor, Lauren's computer sat disassembled next to her TV and a garbage bag full of shoes. Adding to the confusion, Liza's battered aluminum trunk stood upright against the wall, surrounded by big floppy hats, a feather boa, and an old, red bandbox filled with sheet music. Kimberly knelt on the floor by one of the boxes, taping it shut. Winnie was half-hidden inside Lauren's closet.

Squeak! Squeak! Squeak!

The sound was right outside her room. Lauren appeared in the doorway, wheeling her microwave on a wooden dolly.

"I hope nobody's going to be mad that I'm taking back my oven from the common room," Lauren said.

Faith looked up miserably at her soon-to-be-former roommate. "It's not the microwave we're going to miss."

"Are you sure you want me to just throw all these beautiful clothes into a garbage bag?" Winnie asked Lauren from the closet. "Don't you think we should hang them up, or something?"

Lauren shrugged. "I never wear that stuff anymore anyway, so a few wrinkles aren't going to make any difference."

"Okay," Winnie said dubiously, taking a handful of tweedy, wool blazers off the rod and laying them neatly inside a big, black plastic bag.

"That's the last box!" Kimberly announced, taping it shut. "We can start loading my car."

"It's really nice of you to let me use your car," Lauren said to Kimberly. "I don't know how I would have done this, otherwise. I certainly couldn't have afforded to pay a moving company."

"It's no problem," Kimberly said. "We're not even going a mile. I'm just glad I have the car so I can help you."

"I can't believe you're really going through with this," Faith said for the tenth time to Lauren. "I'm going to miss you *so much.*"

Lauren, who'd started labeling boxes with a thick, black magic marker, stopped what she was doing and came over to give Faith a hug. "I promise you," she said, "we'll still spend lots of time together. Like Kimberly said, it's less than a mile, and it's not like I'm going to a different school."

"But it won't be the same," Faith whispered. "Things have gone so smoothly. Now, with Liza here, I'm afraid . . ."

"When I hear the music, it does something to me . . ." The scratchy voice boomed through the hallway, backed up by sappy sounding violins. It was an old recording of the musical *She's My Baby*. The song grew louder and Liza appeared in the doorway, carrying a boombox and wearing a long, black dress with a chiffon handkerchief hemline, a blue velvet porkpie hat, and silver cowboy boots.

"Hi, Liza!" Faith said, forcing herself to sound friendly. Actually, it didn't matter how she sounded because she could barely hear her voice over the loud music.

Liza ignored Faith and stepped over the boxes and bags on the floor. After dumping the boombox on her unmade bed, she tilted her trunk down to the floor and opened it. First she removed several dozen plastic hair rollers in various colors, then a pair of tap shoes, a bright green stretch minidress, and a bathing cap with floppy daisies attached to it. Faith almost expected Liza to pull out a magic carpet or a rubber chicken next.

While Liza was unpacking, Lauren stacked her boxes on the dolly. Kimberly lifted the two garbage bags of clothes and shoes, and Winnie picked up the television.

"I've got someone holding the service elevator," Winnie shouted over the music. "I think we should load everything on at once."

"I'll help you," Kimberly yelled, "then I'll take the stairs and bring the car around to the back entrance."

"I'll be right back to say goodbye," Lauren promised as she pushed the stack of boxes away on the dolly, followed by Winnie and Kimberly.

Faith watched with a sinking heart as Lauren's possessions were carted away and Liza's spread out over the empty space. Liza started singing along with her boombox, in her atonal voice.

"When I hear the music, I'm not scared to chance it

I'll sing it, romance it,
I know I can dance it . . ."

Why, oh *why,* had Lauren happened to mention her problem in the theater in front of Liza? Of all the people in the world who could have taken Lauren's place, why did it have to be someone who seemed determined to make her life miserable? How was Faith supposed to spend the rest of the semester with someone who wasn't even speaking to her—or even worse, someone who was trying to drive her out of her own room?

Winnie and Kimberly reappeared and loaded Lauren's computer on the dolly. Then Kimberly took Lauren's two matching designer suitcases, Winnie wheeled the computer away, and there was nothing left of Lauren except Lauren herself, standing in the hall. Well-mannered, soft-spoken, comfortable Lauren, waiting to say goodbye, her violet eyes filled with tears.

"Oh, Lauren!" Faith cried, running out to the hall to give her friend one last hug goodbye.

Lauren hugged her back and sniffled. "I know I keep saying I'll be so close," she finally admitted, "but it feels like I'm moving to a foreign country!"

"That's almost how I feel," Faith said, "and I haven't even gone anywhere."

"You'll be okay," Lauren said, patting Faith's hair. "And so will I."

"Right," Faith said in a shaky voice.

"Lauren!" Winnie called from the end of the hall, poking her head out of the elevator. "Someone else needs to use this downstairs."

"I've got to go," Lauren said, a tear rolling down her face.

Faith planted a kiss on Lauren's damp cheek. "Call me tonight," she said. "Tell me how much you love your new place."

"You'll have to come see it," Lauren said, backing down the hall and blowing a kiss. Then she turned and ran to the elevator. "I'm coming, you guys!" she shouted.

Faith took a deep breath before venturing back into her noisy, overflowing room. How could she go in there with Liza practically ready to scratch her eyes out for not giving her a part in the show? Maybe KC or Winnie would let Faith sleep on their floor for a couple of days, or maybe for a few months.

But that wasn't the way to handle the problem. She couldn't avoid Liza forever. She had to figure out some other way to make peace, or at least call a truce between them. As Faith stepped timidly into her room, she tried to figure out what she could say or do to Liza that would put her in a better mood. But aside from giving Liza a part in her show, Faith couldn't think of anything. Then it hit her. Liza could be the next best thing to being one of the stars—she could be an understudy! That should pacify her. Faith could ask Liza to be Kimberly's understudy. That would give Liza something to do in the show, but at no risk to Faith or the Follies. Kimberly was extremely dependable.

"Liza?" Faith asked, wading through the plastic rollers, sheet music, and polka dot pajamas with feet. "I wonder if you could do me a big favor."

Liza gave Faith a look that plainly said "Drop dead." Faith was quaking inside, but she was determined not to give up.

"You seem to know 'When I Hear the Music' so well," Faith continued, "so I was wondering if you'd be available to understudy the song."

"Understudy?" Liza sniffed, but there was a gleam of interest in her blue eyes.

"Of course, it would be fairly demanding," Faith improvised. "You'd have to attend every rehearsal and learn all the choreography and be ready to go on at a moment's notice. I realize that's a lot to ask of anyone, so I'd understand if you weren't willing to do it."

"Let me check my book," Liza said self-importantly, opening a leopard-striped covered binder. "Hmm . . . Tuesday . . . Thursday . . . yes, it seems like I might be available then."

"Great!" Faith said. "You'd really be saving my life. I mean, having someone as talented as you,

even as a back-up, makes me feel a lot more secure."

Liza allowed herself a tiny smile. "Well, it's all
for the good of show biz."

As Lauren climbed the stairs, struggling under
the weight of her TV set, she struggled to hold
back tears. One eleven Neptune Avenue, the
funky, bohemian place she remembered from a
few days ago, had vanished. It had been replaced
by a dingy, narrow building with dirty bricks and
dimly lit hallways and a wino lying passed out in
the vestibule. How could she have been so blind
and so stupid? She'd been so desperate to find a
place that she hadn't even looked anywhere else.
And now she had to pay the price. She'd given all
her money to Mrs. Calvin, so she had to stay
here whether she liked it or not.

Panting and sweating, Lauren reached the
fourth floor. Shifting the TV to one arm, she
unlocked the black steel front door and pushed it
open. She wanted to put the TV down, but then
noticed that the puddle of water under the refrigerator had spread over the entire living room
floor. Even worse, the kitchen's cracked linoleum, which was completely submerged, had
curled up around the edges. Then Lauren noticed something floating in the water. It was a

giant cockroach. Only it wasn't dead. It was swimming.

"How's it look?" Winnie asked, as she and Kimberly entered the apartment behind Lauren, carrying various pieces of Lauren's computer.

Lauren stared dully at her new home. Then she burst into tears.

Twelve

"**I** can't believe we finally worked out the logistics of this," KC said to Faith over the Langston House hall phone, Saturday afternoon. "Between your non-stop rehearsals and all the work I've been doing over at Tri Beta to help set up for the ceremony tonight, I thought we'd never find a time and a place."

"Well, I don't have *much* time," Faith said. "My rehearsal starts at three."

"No problem," KC said. "Sheldon's waiting for me downstairs right now. I'll just walk him over to your dorm, and the rest will be history. You can name your children after me."

"Kahia Cayanne Copperstein," Faith laughed.

"If we had a boy, I'm sure he'd love being called that."

"What are you wearing?" KC asked.

"I'm pretty casual. Just a jeans skirt, a striped, cotton blouse, and my cowboy boots. Oh, and I did my hair in a French braid. Big surprise."

KC laughed. "You sound like your usual cute self. Okay, now don't move a muscle. We'll be over there in five minutes."

"I'm glued to my chair," Faith said. "I just hope I can think of something to say to him."

"You'll be fine," KC assured her. "Bye."

KC hung up the phone, dashed through the hall and down the wooden stairs with the mahogany railing. Sheldon stood by the front door. He wore a black leather motorcycle jacket, gray, wool slacks, and his black, snakeskin loafers. His wavy hair was mussed, which made him look even more attractive than usual. Faith was going to die when she saw him.

"Hi!" KC said as she bounded up to him.

Sheldon grimaced uncomfortably.

"What's the matter?" KC asked him.

Sheldon shrugged. "I'm just not too good with blind date situations. I never know what to say."

"It's easy!" KC said, pushing open the door

leading to the porch. "Just say whatever you'd normally say to someone you already know."

"But that's entirely different," Sheldon pointed out as they passed through the porch and down the steps to the green. "When you already know someone, you have some idea what their interests are. You don't run the risk of asking questions for which there are no answers."

"What are you talking about?" KC asked. "What kind of questions have no answers?"

"For example," Sheldon said, "what if I ask her if she has any brothers or sisters, but she's an only child? That would be potentially embarrassing."

"No it wouldn't," KC said. "She'd just say she doesn't have any. But in this case, she'd say that she does, because Faith *does* have a sister."

"You see what I mean?" Sheldon said, shoving his hands in his pockets and frowning. "It can get very complicated."

"Sheldon, Sheldon," KC said in a jocular voice. "You've got to loosen up. You'll do fine! Trust me!"

"I believe I'm feeling an excess of tension," Sheldon said. "I can always tell because my neck gets stiff and my shoulders ache."

"That's easy to fix," KC said as she and Sheldon approached the entrance to Coleridge Hall. "Stop right there."

Sheldon paused and KC stood behind him. "My mother taught me this," KC said, pressing her thumbs into the back of Sheldon's neck and massaging with a firm, circular motion. "I think she learned it on a trip to India back in the sixties."

"Ohhhh," Sheldon moaned, letting his head slump forward. "That feels great!"

After several moments, KC stopped. Sheldon lifted his head and smiled.

"Feeling better?" KC asked.

"Much," Sheldon said, pushing open the front door to Coleridge Hall. The smell of paint and turpentine assaulted their nostrils. As they turned left, KC saw half a dozen students in tattered overalls standing on a tarp with paintbrushes and spray cans. They were painting a colorful, freeform mural on the wall.

"I've never had anyone rub my neck like that before," Sheldon said as they walked down the hall. "You must have magic fingers!"

"Whatever I can do to relax you," KC said. "I'm at your service."

"Of course, I'm still a little tense," Sheldon admitted.

"Then there's only one thing to do," KC said with a serious look.

"What's that?"

KC began to tickle the back of Sheldon's neck.

Sheldon started laughing. "Stop that, KC! You're driving me crazy!"

"Are you loose?" KC demanded. "Or am I going to have to resort to more drastic measures?"

"I'm relaxed! I'm relaxed!" Sheldon said.

"This way," KC said, pulling on the pocket of Sheldon's jacket. She led him up the staircase, and turned right once they reached the second floor landing. "Now don't worry," KC said as she stopped in front of Faith's door and knocked. "Faith is very easy to talk to. You're going to have a wonderful time."

Sheldon nodded curtly as the door opened. Faith stood in the doorway, smiling shyly. Sheldon looked down at her, then looked at KC uncertainly as if to say "What do I do now?"

"Sheldon," KC said, guiding his right hand toward Faith, "this is my friend Faith Crowley. Faith, Sheldon."

Faith took Sheldon's hand and nodded. "Nice to meet you."

"Aren't you going to invite us in?" KC asked.

"Of course." Faith stepped back so KC and Sheldon could enter.

The room looked completely different from the last time KC had seen it. Or at least half of it did. KC recognized the patchwork quilt on Faith's bed and the old teddy bear with the suspenders and the felt hat. But the rest of the room looked like a costume shop! A dozen hats, some with veils, some with plastic fruit attached, hung on the wall. On the floor beneath the hats were several rows of funky shoes, including platform sandals, fuzzy pink bunny slippers, purple sneakers, and silver cowboy boots.

"I guess your new roommate's here," KC said drily.

Faith nodded. "But fortunately she's not in the room at the moment. Do you guys want to sit down?"

"Actually," KC said, "I've got to go to Tri Beta. Courtney's going to lend me a dress for the Gamma dance tonight, and I have to try it on."

Faith's eyes widened in alarm. KC knew Faith didn't want to be left alone with Sheldon, who hovered uncertainly near the door. But KC knew if she stuck around, she'd end up carrying the whole conversation. The only way to get them talking was to leave.

"See you guys!" KC called gaily, waving as she dashed out the door.

As Faith watched KC go, she felt abandoned

and a little bit silly. What was she supposed to say to him? Sure, he was gorgeous, but all she knew about him was his name. She had to try, though. She owed it to KC, and to herself. She couldn't let her work consume her to the point where she didn't have any social life.

"Sheldon?" Faith asked. "Would you like some tea? I've got tea bags and a heating coil."

"Aren't those against dorm regulations?" Sheldon asked. "I believe it was on page seventeen of the freshman manual. No heating coils, no hot plates. Microwave ovens, however, are permissible."

"Sorry," Faith said. "I don't have a microwave. I hope you're not going to turn me in to the authorities for possession of a concealed heating coil."

"No!" Sheldon said generously. "I think we can let this one slide."

"Thanks," Faith said.

Sheldon remained near the door, shifting from one foot to another. He wasn't making this any easier. Faith tried to forget about her own discomfort and focus on making Sheldon feel more relaxed.

"Would you like to take off your jacket and sit down?" Faith asked.

"Sure," Sheldon said, removing his jacket and

folding it neatly over his arm. Then he looked around in confusion. "Where shall I sit?"

"Why don't you take the desk chair," Faith said, sitting on the bed.

Sheldon sat down and Faith studied him for a moment. She could definitely see why KC had been so excited about him. He was super handsome.

"So tell me something about yourself," Faith said pleasantly. "Where are you from?"

"Do you mean where do my parents live or where was I born?" Sheldon asked.

"Is there a difference?"

"Few children are born at home these days," Sheldon said. "I was born at Wildwood Hospital, but my parents live at 43 Wilputte Place in Wildwood."

"Very interesting," Faith said, trying not to laugh. She didn't know what to ask him next.

"So I hear you have a sister," Sheldon said.

Faith nodded. "Marlee. She's sixteen."

Sheldon nodded too. "I see."

Faith checked her watch. It was almost two o'clock. She'd have to leave for rehearsal soon.

"I don't want to keep you if there's somewhere you have to go," Sheldon said.

Faith felt bad. She hadn't meant to make Sheldon feel unwelcome even if they *didn't* have anything to say to each other. Not that she'd really given him a chance. Five minutes was hardly enough time to get to know somebody.

"Look," Faith said, "I really *do* have to go. I'm directing a show and we have rehearsal in a little while. But we're having a party here Friday night after the show is over. Would you like to come?"

"I don't go to many parties," Sheldon said somberly, "but I shouldn't limit the scope of my experience."

"Does that mean yes?" Faith asked.

Sheldon nodded. "Where and when?" he asked, pulling a black leather organizer out of the pocket of his leather jacket.

"Friday night around eleven o'clock," Faith said. "In the dorm lobby."

Sheldon wrote down the information in neat, tiny letters. "I'll see you there," he said, rising and putting on his jacket.

Peter closed the door to his darkroom and backed up against the ledge that held his developing trays. He looked at his shaking hands, blood red under his red worklight. He felt like his heart had just been ripped out of his chest. He wanted to scream, but no sound came out.

He hadn't wanted to believe the girl in KC's dorm when she'd told him about KC and the good-looking guy. He'd wanted to give KC the benefit of the doubt. Maybe the guy was just a friend. Maybe the girl had been exaggerating. But after what he had just seen in the lobby, Peter knew his worst fears had come true.

He'd been working in his darkroom when he'd heard KC's voice. Wanting to jump out and surprise her, Peter had opened the door a crack, only to see KC fondling some stud who perfectly matched the description that the girl had given him. Obviously KC cared so little about Peter that she wasn't even trying to hide it when she was running around with other guys.

How many times do you have to play the fool before it finally sinks in? demanded an angry voice inside him. *When are you going to learn? Girls like KC just don't breathe the same air as ordinary slobs like you. Girls like that go out with guys like that—guys who look good in front of the camera, not guys who hide behind it. She dumped you at Winter Formal to go out with a pretty boy, so it should come as no surprise that she's doing it again.*

Peter drew in a shaky breath and steadied himself against the ledge. Part of him wanted to stay in the darkroom for the rest of his life. He belonged in the dark where no one else could see what a fool he was.

But of course that wasn't an option. He'd have

to go out there eventually and face her again. Or, rather, watch her go skipping off on the arm of another guy. And there wasn't a thing he could do about it. Except not let her know how much it hurt. Yes, that would be his strategy. When he saw her again, he wouldn't mention the pretty boy. He'd act like nothing had ever happened between KC and him. He'd act like she was just a casual acquaintance. He'd be so cool and unimpressed that KC would wonder if he even remembered her name.

Thirteen

KC felt like she should be wearing glass slippers. Her long, white dress was fitted through the bodice, then full in the skirt, reaching almost to the floor. The sheer, puffy sleeves were short, exposing her slender arms. In addition to lending her this dress for the Saturday night Gamma party, Courtney had gathered KC's hair up in a loose knot, with curly tendrils escaping around her face.

Overhead, crystal chandeliers of the Gamma house living room cast a sparkly, silver light on the elegantly dressed partygoers below. KC's sorority sisters, always well-dressed, had outdone themselves tonight. They were a sea of designer gowns, sequins, and strapless sheaths exposing polished shoulders and long necks. Their dates, no less dazzling, wore tuxedos or tastefully somber suits with silk ties. Though KC had told herself over and over again not to worry about what Peter would be wearing, she couldn't help hoping that at least he'd show up in a decent jacket and tie. That way he'd still be underdressed, but at least presentable.

KC tilted her face up to the shimmering light of the chandeliers. She felt like the whole evening had been bathed in light. It had started with the glowing candles of the ceremony earlier at Tri Beta house, where each Tri Beta, old and new, had promised loyalty and friendship to her sisters. Then there was the moonlit, starlit walk along Greek row as KC and her new sisters made their way to the party. Soon it would end with spotlights, when all the pledges and their dates would be presented to the rest of the party.

"KC!" Courtney called to her from halfway across the living room, waving above several sleekly-styled hairdos.

KC waved back excitedly. It was hard to talk over the hum of conversation and the music of the live string quartet.

Courtney began to push her way through the crowd, followed by a sweet-faced guy with long, dark hair. The guy looked around him with wide-eyed wonder. He certainly didn't look at home, and with a black Grateful Dead T-shirt, black jeans, and black sneakers on, he stood out from everyone else. His only concession to the party was an antique, black tuxedo jacket and a bright red bowtie, which stood out starkly against his bare neck. He was Courtney's date, Phoenix Cates.

"Hi, you guys!" KC said as Courtney and Phoenix found an empty spot to stand in. "Are you having fun?"

Courtney nodded. "Yes, but I think Phoenix is a little overwhelmed."

"I didn't know anyone our age dressed like this," Phoenix admitted. "I almost feel like I'm crashing my parents' party or something."

"We can go anytime after I introduce my new sisters," Courtney said. "Just say the word."

"Nope," Phoenix said. "As long as you want to be here, that's where I want to be." Phoenix wrapped his arms around Courtney and planted a kiss on her cheek.

"Is he great or what?" Courtney asked, grinning happily at KC.

"He's great," KC agreed, envying the ease Courtney felt with a date who was so obviously not cut out of the fraternity mold. But that was because Courtney felt secure in her social position. No matter what she did, she would still be accepted by the best people. KC couldn't wait for the day she could feel that way. Then she could invite Peter anywhere without worrying about what people would think.

So where *was* Peter? KC checked her watch. It was ten after ten. KC had made it very clear to him that new pledges were being presented at ten-thirty.

"Where's Peter?" Courtney asked, echoing KC's thoughts. "Raiding the hors d'oeuvres table?"

"I guess he's just a little late," KC said. "I'm sure he'll be here any minute."

Courtney nodded. "I've posted Diane Woo by the front door to guide all the new pledges and their dates. We can give her a description of Peter and have her tell him to meet us at the top of the staircase when we line up for the presentation. I'd better start rounding up people now so we'll be all lined up by ten-thirty."

"I think I'll wait by the front door," KC said. "That way it will be easier for Peter when he walks in. I'll just grab him and bring him upstairs myself."

"Sure," Courtney said. "We'll see you up there. Come on, Phoenix." Grabbing his hand, Courtney headed for a cluster of new Tri Beta pledges talking excitedly by the punch bowl. "It's time, everyone," she said.

KC slid gracefully through the crowd toward the front entrance hall. Diane Woo, the Tri Beta secretary, stood by the double-width front door with its oversized brass doorknob. She wore a simple, sleeveless black velvet dress. Diamond stud earrings peeped out from beneath her shoulder-length black hair.

"Diane," KC said, going up to the senior, "has a guy named Peter Dvorsky walked in yet? He's my date for tonight."

"Let me check my list," Diane said. Her glossy, straight hair fell forward over her face as she looked at her clipboard. "No, not yet."

KC sighed. What could be keeping Peter? He'd never been flaky or undependable before, and there was no way he'd stand her up. There had to be some other explanation. Could he have forgotten about the dance or mixed up the night? It wasn't likely. She'd just spoken to him a few days ago, and he'd been the one to bring up the dance. He'd even sounded excited about it. So where was he?

A few minutes later, Courtney appeared in the front hall and placed a gentle hand on KC's shoulder. "I know you want to wait down here," she said kindly, "but everyone else is lined up upstairs."

KC bit her lip. "I don't know what to do!" she said to Courtney. "Peter would never be late. I'm afraid something might have happened to him."

"I'm sure that's not it," Courtney said. "All kinds of things could have come up. I bet he'll come running through that door any second now." She turned to Diane. "And when he does, tell him to go through the kitchen and up the back stairs. Come on, KC."

KC allowed herself to be led up the sweeping staircase with its deep, red Oriental carpet. At the top, a double row of evening gowned beauties and their handsome escorts snaked down the long hallway. The last six girls on line were the new Tri Beta pledges. Phoenix sat cross-legged on a bench in the hall, absorbed in a book of poetry.

"I switched the order of the sororities," Courtney whispered to KC. "Now we're going last, just to give Peter more time to get here."

"Thanks," KC said, "but he's already had plenty of time to get here. I'm *sure* something happened to him. Something horrible. That's the only explanation. Maybe he had an accident in his darkroom. Maybe one of those heavy pieces of equipment fell on him, or maybe he spilled one of his solutions on himself. All those dangerous chemicals . . ." KC pictured Peter lying on the floor of his darkroom, scalded and helpless, and she began to have trouble breathing.

"Calm down," Courtney said, soothingly. "I'm sure he's fine."

"But if he's fine, he would have called here, or gotten a message to me somehow," KC insisted, her voice rising. "Maybe I should call the campus police! No, they'll never find him. I should go look for him myself. You'd understand, wouldn't you, if I didn't go through with this presentation? I mean, you know how much Tri Beta means to me, but this could be a matter of life and death!"

"You're blowing this way out of proportion," Courtney said. "I promise you, any minute now he's going to come dashing up the back stairs with a perfectly reasonable explanation."

"Well, I might not be able to do the presentation anyway," KC said. "If Peter gets here too late, I won't have an escort. I can't walk down the stairs by myself."

"Hmmm . . ." Courtney surveyed the upstairs hall while she thought about that. "I'm sure we can find you a stand-in, just in case." Her eyes fell upon Phoenix, who was dreamily turn-ing the pages of his poetry book. "Aha!" she said.

No, KC thought to herself. *Not Phoenix!* While part of her was honored that Courtney Connor, Tri Beta president, was giving her her own date, the rest of her was picturing what she'd look like walking down the stairs on the arm of this long-haired guy! What would the other sorority and fraternity members think of her?

That I like hanging out with hippies, KC thought with some irony. *Which isn't that far from the truth. Why is it that no matter how far I get from my parents and my upbringing, it always seems to haunt me?* And to think she'd been worried about how she'd look with Peter on her arm! But all her worries seemed silly now, compared with the ag-ony of wondering what had happened to Peter.

"It's ten twenty-nine," Courtney said. "I don't think we can afford to wait any longer."

KC nodded grimly, and Courtney went over to talk to Phoenix. Well, at least Phoenix was a male. That was better than no escort at all.

Phoenix appeared at KC's side. "Hi!" he said cheerfully. "I guess you and me are going for a little walk."

The chandeliers dimmed and a white spotlight shone on Courtney, picking up the highlights in her golden hair.

"Ladies and gentlemen of Greek row," she said, "this year I have the pleasure of presenting to you your new brothers and sisters! First, the pledges of Omega Delta Tau. May I introduce Mr. Geoffrey Whitley and his escort, Miss Bridget Porter!"

As the line inched forward, KC kept checking over her shoulder, hoping desperately that Peter would appear, breathless, in the hall. Even if he showed up in sweatpants and a T-shirt, she'd be happy to see him. She just wanted to know he was safe and sound.

". . . and, finally, the new sisters of Beta Beta Beta. May I introduce Miss Lisa Jean McDermott and her escort, Mr. Charles Lawrence!"

There were only a few couples left in front of her. It was time KC faced the truth. Peter wasn't coming. He was probably dead, or at the very least maimed beyond recognition. What a cruel joke life was. One minute you could be happily going about your business, the next minute something horrible happened to take away someone you cared about. This was exactly like the time KC and Faith had waited for Winnie at the bus station to go home for Thanksgiving. Winnie had never showed up, and it was because she'd been in a major automobile accident. Something even worse could have happened to Peter.

Just the thought of it made KC's legs start to buckle.

". . . Miss Kahia Cayanne Angeletti, and her escort, Phoenix Cates."

"C'mon," Phoenix whispered. "I'll help you down."

KC forced her lips into a smile as she took Phoenix's arm with one hand and clutched the brass railing with the other. Her legs felt numb, but she somehow managed to get to the bottom of the stairs without falling. As they reached the bottom step, to light applause, KC gave Phoenix a quick thanks. Then, on wobbly legs, she struggled through the crowd.

"Any sign of Peter?" she asked, finding Diane.

Diane shook her head regretfully.

The chandeliers came back on and the crowd in the hallway moved back into the living room. Courtney came down the stairs, looking around anxiously for KC.

"Well?" Courtney asked when KC met her at the bottom of the stairs.

"He's still not here," KC said. "I've got to go look for him. I'd never forgive myself if something happened to him and I didn't try to help him."

Courtney nodded. "Do you want me to come with you?"

KC shook her head. "I'll call you if I need help. And thanks for the dress and the date and everything else."

"You're welcome," Courtney said. "Now go! Get out of here! I hope Peter's okay."

With a cheerless smile, KC pushed through evening gowns and tuxedos, and ran out into the night. The sky was dark and clear, and the stars shone brightly overhead. Crickets chirped peacefully as if all was well. But something was very, very wrong. Peter was in trouble, and KC had to find him.

The most logical place to start was his dorm, Coleridge Hall. Even if he wasn't there, maybe one of his neighbors would have some idea where he'd gone. As KC ran across the green, her high heels sank into the grass, slowing her down. Not wanting to waste another second, KC took off her shoes and ran barefoot over the cool, damp earth.

When she reached Coleridge Hall, she yanked open the door and nearly collided with two young men. They wore black tights, turtlenecks, and white face paint. One was leaning against an imaginary wall, and the other sat on a chair that wasn't there, drinking from an invisible teacup.

"Sorry!" KC yelled.

"Looks like Cinderella lost her slippers," one mime said to the other as KC ran down the hall.

"And her prince," the other observed as he poured himself another invisible cup of tea.

KC knocked on Peter's door. "Peter!" she cried. "It's KC! Are you in there?"

There was no answer. Maybe he was in the darkroom. KC ran a few steps further down the hall and banged on the darkroom door. To her surprise, the door opened and Peter, safe and healthy, looked at her calmly.

"What's up?" he asked.

"What's up???" KC shouted. "I thought you were killed or seriously injured!"

"Why would you think that?" Peter asked.

"Why do you think?" KC demanded. "You didn't show up at the dance tonight. What other explanation could there be?"

"I hardly think death or serious injury are the only reasons someone wouldn't go to a sorority party," Peter said. "I mean, maybe those are the only things that would hold *you* back, but some of us have other priorities."

"Huh?" KC asked, dazed at Peter's flip and casual attitude. "Did you forget we had a date?"

"I know you said something about a party," Peter said, as if he was trying to remember, "but I didn't think it was that big a deal." Peter walked back into the darkroom. "Anyway, I had some important work I wanted to catch up on."

KC followed Peter inside and watched as he pulled out a dripping sheet of paper from one of the trays. The photograph, already developed, looked familiar. It was a girl's face from one of the pictures Peter had taken for last semester's Classic Calendar. The calendar wasn't being sold anymore. What was so important about that?

"Peter," KC pleaded, almost in tears, "I don't understand. Why are you doing this to me?"

"I'm not doing a thing to you," Peter said calmly, hanging the wet photograph on a string with a clothespin. "I'm just minding my own business. Why is it you think everything everyone does has something to do with you? That's a very self-centered view of the universe."

KC choked back a sob and stared at Peter, hoping he'd offer some explanation for his behavior. But he ignored her, working cheerfully in the red light. After another moment, KC couldn't stand it anymore. Without a word, she turned and headed back down the hall, still carrying her shoes.

Fourteen

I know this isn't much," Faith said on Friday afternoon of the next week. She was carrying a tray of cookies and soda into the costume room of the U. of S. theater. "But I just wanted to thank you all for helping me today. Everyone in the theater department's going crazy getting ready for the show tonight, so there's no one else to help me with my costumes. And I should have known better than to volunteer to handle the programs. I didn't realize each and every one of them would have to be folded by hand."

"I'll do anything for a chocolate chip cookie," Winnie said from where she sat on a folding chair, sewing sequins onto a fringed flapper dress. As Faith put the tray down on a table near her, Winnie pulled a cookie out of the box and bit into it. "Ahhh," she sighed as she chewed with pleasure.

"And don't thank me," Lauren said from where she sat, cross-legged, on the floor folding programs. "I'm so glad to have an excuse to see everybody I practically ran over here. I just wish I could see the show tonight, but I've got to scrub toilets at the Springfield Inn."

"I certainly had nothing else to do," KC said. "I'm all caught up with my homework, Tri Beta's got nothing scheduled for tonight, and I certainly didn't have a *date."* She sighed as she sewed, reattaching a sleeve to a tuxedo jacket. The jacket was going to be worn by the male singer in the love duet of Faith's segment of the show.

"Well, thanks to KC, *I* have a date," Faith said. "I invited Sheldon to meet me at the cast party in Coleridge tonight after the show. You're coming to the party, aren't you, Kimberly?"

Kimberly, who sat in a wide straddle on the floor beside Lauren, folding programs, shrugged noncommittally.

"You want something to drink, Kim?" Faith

asked, kneeling down beside her with a cup of water.

Kimberly shook her head. "I'm not thirsty."

"But you should drink something," Faith insisted. "You rehearsed all morning and you've got a performance tonight. You don't want to get dehydrated."

"Mother Faith," Winnie commented as she sewed.

Kimberly sighed and took the cup. After taking a small sip, she put it down and continued folding programs in thirds, as Faith had requested.

"You okay, Kim?" Faith asked, observing the stony expression on Kimberly's face. "You seem tired."

"I'm fine," Kimberly said tersely.

Faith knew Kimberly was upset about something, but she couldn't figure out what. And no matter how many times she asked, Kimberly wouldn't tell her. Had Faith been working her too hard? Faith really hadn't had any choice, given how little time they had to put the show together. And no one else in the show had complained.

Actually, Kimberly hadn't complained, either. Faith was just guessing. All she knew was that as the day of the show drew closer, Kimberly had seemed more and more tense. At least her song and dance number looked good. Maybe after the show, they could sit down and talk about what was bothering her.

At least Faith didn't have to worry about Liza anymore. Her new roommate had come to every rehearsal, even for the numbers she wasn't understudying. She'd learned the words to every song, and every bit of the choreography, eyeing the other performers hungrily, jealously, as if she couldn't wait to leap on them and steal their part away. And every time Faith complimented anyone, especially Kimberly, Liza would glare at Faith resentfully, as if to say "I could have done it better." But the show would be starting in just a few hours, and all Faith's performers were in perfect health. So Liza would have to be content to hover backstage. Faith sat down on the floor beside Lauren and took a handful of programs off the huge stack. "Wow," she said, seeing how many programs were still left to fold, "I didn't realize you guys would end up doing the whole thing. I know it's a lot."

"Dash wanted to come help, too," Lauren said, "but he has to spend the weekend catching up on his schoolwork. His journalism seminar has taken up so much time."

"How is Dash?" Winnie asked.

Lauren paused in her folding and looked at Winnie with troubled, violet eyes. "I haven't seen him much since he started taking this master class. It's been kind of lonely. My apartment's so out of the way."

"How is it shaping up?" KC asked as she poked her needle through the tuxedo sleeve and drew it up again. "I'm sorry I haven't had time to come visit you in your new place."

"It's not much to look at," Lauren admitted. "I was trying to tell myself that it was chic and bohemian, but the truth is, it's a real dump. I get depressed every time I walk in the door."

"I feel afraid every time I walk into my dorm," Winnie said. "With all the frisbees, footballs, and human cannonballs flying through the air, I need a crash helmet just to get through the lobby."

"Well, at least you have Josh," KC said. "You can always seek refuge in his room."

"I wish," Winnie said sadly. "The last time we tried to do that, someone stole his furniture! And would you believe we still haven't talked about our relationship? At this point, I'm not even sure we have a relationship. We're just two ships, crashing in the night."

"Ouch!" KC cried suddenly, raising her finger to her mouth and sucking on it.

"What's the matter?" Faith asked, looking up

from where she sat on the floor. "Did you prick yourself?"

KC nodded and held up the offending needle, attached by a thread to the tuxedo jacket. She removed the finger from her mouth. "I guess I should be more careful—especially when I get involved with men."

Faith reached up and patted KC's knee. "You still haven't talked to Peter?"

KC shook her head and her lower lip quivered. "It's been a week since Peter ditched me," she said in a choked voice, as tears started spilling down her face, "and I still don't have a clue why he did it. The last time we got together he took pictures of me for a class assignment. We had a great time and we even kissed. Was he just setting me up for a fall?" KC sniffled and tried to wipe the tears away with her hand, but they were coming too fast.

Faith found a large scrap of material in the sewing kit and gently mopped up KC's cheeks. "There's got to be some other reason why Peter acted that way," she said, trying to comfort KC. "I was sure he really liked you. It was in his eyes every time you were together."

"I notice you're talking in the past tense," KC said wretchedly, taking the scrap of material from Faith and patting her face with it. "But how can

Peter and I already be in the past tense when we never had a present? We didn't even have a fight or a disagreement." KC began to cry even harder.

"You don't know that for sure," Kimberly said. "Until you talk to him, face-to-face, you won't know what's really going on."

"I've tried!" KC insisted. "I've tried to talk to him a couple of times in the dining commons, and he completely ignored me."

"He's obviously playing some sort of game," Winnie said.

Faith shook her head. "I never would have taken him for a game player. He strikes me as such a down-to-earth guy."

"That's what I thought," KC said, her voice hoarse. "I'm never trusting a guy again!" She hid her face in her hands, and her whole body shook as she sobbed.

"Oh boy." Faith looked from sobbing KC to Winnie, who was eating handful after handful of chocolate chip cookies, to depressed Lauren, to silent Kimberly. "We sure are a happy group."

Just before eight o'clock that night, Meredith banged on the door of the women's dressing room. "Five minutes, please. Five minutes!" he called.

Five minutes to the end of the world, Kimberly

thought, stiffening at the sound of Meredith's voice. Tick, tick, tick. Second by second, the clock was bringing Kimberly closer to the moment when the axe would fall. If only there were some way she could stop time so she'd never have to go on. How could she dance when she couldn't even move?

Kimberly's hand, which held an eyeliner brush, had frozen on its way up to her eyelid. She stared at herself in the brightly lit makeup mirror. She wore a pale, orange chiffon dress, a leftover from a show done several years ago. Her brown eyes, with flecks of amber, were wide and frightened. Her thin face looked sunken under the cheekbones.

It's just nerves, she tried to tell herself. *It's normal stagefright. I'm sure every other girl in this dressing room feels the same way.*

Looking into the long mirror, Kimberly saw the reflections of excited girls, patting on pancake makeup, applying false eyelashes, and reinforcing hairdos with hairspray and bobbypins. They chattered with each other, zipped up each other's glittery costumes, strapped on tap shoes, murmured lines to themselves. They seemed nervous, but it was a happy kind of nervous, as if they couldn't wait to go on.

On the other side of the room, Kimberly could

see Freya strolling casually past racks of costumes, hats, and shoes; she wore a long, Victorian dress with a bustle.

"Ahhhhh. Ohhhhhh. Eeeeeee," Freya vocalized, her strong soprano lost in the giddy blur of voices. Catching Kimberly's eye in the mirror, she smiled and waggled her fingers.

"Are you nervous?" Kimberly asked, almost hopefully.

Freya shrugged. "Excited, mostly. I know I shall perform well. I am well-rehearsed."

It must be nice to have so much self-confidence, Kimberly thought. *Although I guess it's easy when you're gifted with such a beautiful voice.*

But you have a gift, too, her mother's voice reminded her as it always did before the annual recital at the Houston Modern Dance Academy. Every year, Kimberly went through the same anxiety attack. It always started about a week before she had to go on stage, and it always followed the same pattern. First she'd have trouble breathing. A few nights before the recital, she'd stop sleeping. Then, besides worrying about performing, she'd worry about the fact that she wasn't sleeping. The only reason she was able to perform at all was that by showtime she was too tired to be nervous.

Now Kimberly was afraid she wouldn't even be

able to do that. Not in front of all those people. Winnie and KC were out there, and Winnie's roommate Melissa, and Melissa's boyfriend Brooks. Not to mention all the bigwigs from the drama and dance departments. And Faith. Kind, sweet Faith who had so much confidence in her.

There was another knock on the door. "Places, please! Places, everyone!" Meredith called.

Kimberly clutched the edge of the makeup table and tried to disappear. Maybe she could just evaporate into thin air. That would solve all her problems. But her gaunt reflection kept on staring back at her with doleful eyes.

Three girls in flapper dresses jumped up from their seats in front of the long make-up mirror, scattering pots of pancake makeup and tubes of mascara.

"I can't believe it's really time!" one of them squealed, making a last-minute check of the sequinned band around her forehead. "How do I look?"

"You look great," Faith answered as she came through the door. Her blond hair was long and loose instead of in the usual French braid, and she wore a black jumper with a lacy, white blouse underneath. "You all look great. Now, there's no time for a last-minute pep talk, so just do as well as you did during rehearsal, and you'll be fine.

Remember that this show is just for kicks. Go out there and have a good time."

"Everything today is thoroughly modern!" the flappers sang giddily as they Charlestoned out the door.

Faith smiled as she watched them leave. "Well, I guess they didn't need me to tell them to have fun," she said to Kimberly. "How about you? Are you ready to have a good time?"

Kimberly tried to smile, but it resembled a grimace.

"I know you're a little nervous," Faith said, "but you're going to be great."

Kimberly nodded silently, hoping that if she believed Faith's words they'd come true.

"Your number is third," Faith said, checking her clipboard. "You have about ten minutes to warm up."

Obediently, Kimberly rose and headed for the door. There was a ballet barre set up backstage so dancers could stretch. Maybe once Kimberly started loosening up, her body would take over and her frantic mind could hide somewhere, deep inside, until her number was over.

"Kimberly," Faith called out as she reached the door. "Break a leg!"

"Thanks," Kimberly said faintly. Break a leg.

That's what her mother always said, too, right before any of her dancers went on.

As Kimberly entered the dimly lit backstage area, she was overwhelmed by the noise and activity. The smell of sawdust mingled with fresh paint, musty costumes, and sweat. Last minute hammering sounds clanged over frenzied voices. Stagehands, dressed in black, ran frantically back and forth across the stage, carrying props and scenery. Meredith stood in the wings just off downstage left, by the lighting board, pushing levers up and down to adjust light levels onstage.

As Kimberly neared the lighting board, she nearly collided with a stagehand rushing past, carrying a ladder. Kimberly leaped back, shaken.

"Better stay out of the way," Meredith warned as he turned up the backstage lights a little. "We don't want any accidents."

With a lump in her throat, Kimberly nodded and ducked behind a black velvet curtain hanging in the wings. From the safety of her hiding place, she could watch everyone without being seen. Onstage, the flappers giggled and fixed each other's hair as they waited for the curtain to rise. A few inches away from Kimberly, Dante Borelli silently mouthed the words to "Trouble in River City." He wore a straw boater hat and a suit with a bow tie. His number was second, right before Kimberly's.

Meredith pulled down a lever labeled House Lights. The murmuring audience, audible backstage, began to quiet down. A loud chord was struck on a piano from the orchestra pit.

"Quiet, please! Quiet everybody," Meredith called to everyone backstage. "Curtain going up!"

The three flappers struck their poses, lips pursed like Kewpie dolls, hands framing their faces. As a stagehand pulled on the ropes to raise the curtain, Meredith pulled on another lever. The lights came up on the flappers and they began to sing the theme from *Thoroughly Modern Millie.*

Well, I'm glad they're having a good time, Kimberly thought as she trudged to the barre, set up in a back corner between some painted, wooden cutout trees and a table set with fake food. Her leg felt heavy as she lifted it onto the barre, and the metal felt cold against her hands. Or maybe her hands were cold. She felt cold all over. Frozen solid. She tried to slide along the barre into a straddle, but her body wouldn't move. After twelve years of dancing and performing, her body had finally rebelled.

What am I doing here? Kimberly asked herself as

her breath started to come in quick gasps. *Why do I put myself through this when it makes me feel this way?*

Because she expects it of you.

She? Faith? Who?

Your mother, of course. The one who bought you ballet slippers before you could even walk. The one who taught you to dance before you could talk. The one who worked with you patiently, for hours, even after a long day with the company. The one who'd be the happiest woman in the world if you took over for her someday, carrying Houston Modern Dance into the next century.

And haven't I done everything she asked? Kimberly agonized. *I've always been everything she's wanted me to be. I've forced myself up on that stage even though it gets harder every year. And I've never complained.*

Good girl, Kimmie honey! Good job! Her mother's voice came again. Or was it Faith's, encouraging her? *Just do your warm-up and you'll be fine. I'm so proud of you!*

The sound of applause broke through the voices in Kimberly's mind. One number down, two to go. Then it would be her turn. Kimberly, the dancing icicle. Not even the stage lights could melt her. Kimberly tried again to slide her leg along the barre but it stayed where it was.

Her hands, too, felt glued in place. Kimberly was afraid that if she let go of the barre, something terrible would happen: she'd fall off the stage into the orchestra pit, a stage light would come crashing down from the ceiling onto her head. No, she couldn't let go of the barre. It was the only thing between her and disaster.

There was another burst of applause. Had the second number ended already? It couldn't be time! Not yet!

"Kimberly!" Faith said, coming up behind her. "You're next!"

Kimberly's body felt so stiff, she couldn't even turn her head to look at Faith.

"Kimberly?" Faith asked, putting a hand on her shoulder. "Are you ready? You've got about thirty seconds."

The world began to spin. Cutout trees and fake food and ladders and flappers swirled around Kimberly's head, making her dizzy. Kimberly was afraid to let go of the barre for fear she'd go spinning off into space.

"I . . . can't . . ." Kimberly managed to croak at Faith.

"You can't what?" Faith asked anxiously. "You can't go on? Are you sick?"

Kimberly was clutching the barre so tightly that she was losing feeling in her fingers.

"What's the problem?" asked a brassy, eager voice, as Liza appeared instantly in front of Kimberly. Even in the half-light her pale white face seemed to radiate energy. She wore a lowcut, bright orange dress that looked like something a barmaid would wear in an old western movie. Her silver cowboy boots peeped out from beneath her petticoats. Kimberly knew it was no coincidence that Liza just happened to be nearby. At every rehearsal, Liza had been lurking around her, just waiting for something like this to happen.

"It's Kimberly," Faith said. "I don't think she can go on. Can you . . ."

"I'm ready!" Liza announced. "How do you like my outfit? It's nothing like what Kimberly's wearing, but it's more me, don't you think? I don't go for those pale colors. Too washed out. I purposely chose this dress because it's almost the same color as my hair."

"Kimberly?" Faith's voice, low and comforting, was in her ear. "Are you sure you can't do it?"

The spinning had slowed down a little, and Kimberly found she was able to speak. "Break a leg," she whispered to Liza.

Liza's dark lips spread into a brilliant smile. "Thanks!" she said. An instant later, she was gone.

The curtain came down on Dante, and Liza took center stage, waiting for her cue. Meredith shot a questioning look at Faith and pointed at Liza. Faith nodded and walked up to the lighting board where Meredith was standing.

"Last minute replacement," Faith muttered to Meredith.

Once again, the stagehand pulled on the ropes, raising the curtain on a pitch black stage. Then a narrow spotlight lit up Liza's pale, angular face with its overblown red lips. As the rinky tink piano music started, the spotlight widened to show Liza's generous body bulging out of the close-fitting orange dress.

"Oh brother," Faith said, turning away from the stage as the musical introduction ended. "I don't think I can watch this."

"When I hear the music . . ." Liza bellowed in her off-key voice, *"it does something to me . . ."*

"Here come the boos," Faith said, tensing her shoulders and closing her eyes. "I hope they don't throw anything at her."

There was silence from the audience. The stagehand manning the ropes snickered. Faith peered around Meredith to see what Liza was doing.

"The tingles shoot through me . . ." Liza wiggled her ample rear end and rolled her eyes like

Mae West. The stagehand snickered again and there were giggles from the audience.

"It feels like a new me!" Liza took little, mincing steps toward the front of the stage, then spread her arms wide, like she was taking in the whole audience. Liza continued to sing even more off key, and her dancing was even worse, but none of it mattered because Liza was funny. As Liza strutted back and forth across the front of the stage, flirting with the audience, and tripping over her own feet, Faith felt a tingle shoot up her own spine. Liza was having a great time out there, and it was contagious. The audience was laughing louder.

"Dancing's like flying. No sighing, no crying, Nothing can touch me up there . . ."

Liza was running around the stage in circles, her arms spread wide like she was an airplane. Meredith and the stagehand were laughing so hard they were clutching their stomachs. Faith could barely hear Liza anymore, so loud was the laughter and applause coming from the audience.

They liked her! They actually liked her! Liza seemed to be feeding off the energy coming from the audience; she seemed almost to glow. There was obviously nowhere else Liza would rather be than up on that stage. Liza's number ended to such tumultuous applause that the stagehand had to lower and raise the curtain three times. Liza wiggled her fanny, blew kisses to the audience, and drank it all in.

"I've never seen anything like it!" Meredith yelled over the cheers. "This is amazing!"

Faith just stared at her new roommate, her mouth open in shock. "I don't believe it," she said quietly. "Liza is a hit!"

Fifteen

"Faith, that was a brilliant move, putting Liza into that number," said Janet Greenberg, a senior and a theater major who'd directed another segment of the show. "I mean, the song is so corny, but by casting against type, you brought out humor I never knew was there!"

Faith could barely hear Janet over the loud rock music blasting over the stereo in the Coleridge Hall lobby, but she could pretty much guess what Janet was saying. Janet was the tenth person at the cast party to congratulate her on Liza's stunning success. Everyone kept saying Faith had made the theatrical discovery of the century, but Faith knew she'd just been incredibly lucky that her cowardly move had paid off so well. Even now, with Liza's performance permanently etched in U. of S. theater history, Faith still couldn't believe it. Was it really possible that Liza had had this comic gift all along and Faith had just been too blind to see it?

At this very moment, Liza was standing on a baby grand piano that one of the music majors had wheeled into the lobby, strutting and wiggling and singing at the top of her lungs over the rock music. The dozens of people gathered around her were laughing and clapping, and an art student was drawing a caricature of her on his easel.

"Faith!" Meredith shouted above the music as he made his way through another large group of dancing performers, many still wearing their exaggerated stage makeup. The flappers, now wearing jeans and sweatshirts, were teaching their dates how to Charleston. Against a newly painted mural on one wall, several folding tables held bottles of soda, bowls of chips, and an enormous sheetcake decorated with a broken leg made out of icing.

"That was quite a coup," Meredith said, as he gave Faith a hug. "I mean, I heard Liza audition. I couldn't understand why you let her understudy Kimberly. I never would have cast her in a singing part. I never would have cast her in anything, if the truth be known. How did you know she'd be so perfect for that number?"

Faith shrugged. She was tired of trying to explain that she didn't deserve any credit. "Director's intuition," she said.

"Faith!" called another voice. Faith turned away from it, not wanting to face another compliment she didn't deserve. "Faith!" the voice called again.

Faith turned to see a tall, muscular young man with dark, wavy hair, green eyes, and impossibly high cheekbones. It was Sheldon Copperstein.

"Hi, Sheldon!" Faith said warmly, although she'd almost forgotten he was coming. "Did you get a chance to see the show?"

Sheldon nodded. "I found it very symmetrical."

"Symmetrical?" Faith asked, trying to comprehend.

"Its structure," Sheldon explained. "The way it was constructed was almost mathematical. Two hours divided by eight directors, for a total of fifteen minutes per director. I'm just curious how such an inexact science as theater could be calculated so precisely."

"I think Meredith was just trying to be fair to

everybody," Faith said, looking around for Meredith, but he'd drifted away with Janet. Faith had a feeling talking wasn't going to be the best way to get to know each other.

"Would you like to dance?" Faith asked.

Sheldon shrugged. "Sure."

Faith took Sheldon's hand and led him toward the other dancers. As they bobbed to the music, Faith noticed that Sheldon was able to keep time. However, he seemed to know only one move. Step front with the right foot, then the left foot. Step back with the right foot, then the left foot. Front, front. Back, back. Right, left. Right, left. Just watching him made Faith start to feel drowsy, as if she were being hypnotized.

After several songs, Faith knew she had to get away from Sheldon, or she'd fall asleep. She'd tried to get to know him. But they had nothing to say to each other. And Sheldon didn't seem to be any more comfortable than she was.

"You know, Sheldon," Faith said finally, "it's been a really long day for me with rehearsal and the show. I think I'm about ready to hit the sack."

Sheldon's face, which had been rigidly focused on his dancing, seemed to relax. "I understand completely," he said. "In fact, I've got to go to sleep myself. I've got an early morning meeting tomorrow with RSACCOA."

"Arsacoa?" Faith asked.

"Rare Stamp and Coin Collectors of America. I'm president of the U. of S. branch," Sheldon said proudly.

"That's great," Faith said. "Good luck."

Spotting a break in the crowd, Faith dashed into it, heading for the door.

There was no way she could escape it. The thumping bass line of the party music traveled up through the floor, making Kimberly's room vibrate. Well, maybe the music was good for the plants. Kimberly had about twenty green, leafy plants of various sizes clustered in pots beneath the window. Dance posters covered her side of the room. A full-length mirror was attached to her closet door, and Kimberly had attached a mini-barre in the middle of it.

Kimberly, lying fully dressed, on her bed, covered her head with her pillow, but even that was not enough to shut out the sound. If she wanted to get away from the cast party, she'd have to leave the dorm. But no matter how far she went, she'd never get away from the humiliating memory of what had happened tonight.

She'd failed. There was no other way to look at it. After battling her nerves all her life, her nerves had finally won. Which left her with nothing to look forward to. The only future she'd ever considered was dancing. But how was she going to be able to dance professionally when she was too scared to get up in front of an audience?

And what was everyone in Coleridge going to say? Now they all knew what a fake she'd been all along. She wasn't a real dancer. She was just a girl who wore legwarmers. Maybe they'd even make her move out of the creative arts dorm since she really didn't belong there. Maybe Lauren would take her in.

But even worse would be telling her mother what had happened. Kimberly reached down to the floor and picked up the letter her mother had written her on Houston Modern Dance Company stationery. The paper crackled as Kimberly unfolded it and reread it:

Kimmie honey,
Just wanted to wish you "Break-a-Leg" on Saturday. I wish I could be there, but duty calls . . .
I know you'll dance like a dream. Call me as soon as it's over. And remember—you'll always be my star.
Love always,
Mom

Some star, thought Kimberly. *More like a falling star.* How was she going to be able to call her mother and give her the bad news? The answer was—she couldn't. Not yet. Maybe she'd be able to figure out something in the morning. Maybe then it would all just seem like a bad dream.

There was a knock on the door. Kimberly really didn't want to answer it. She didn't want to face anybody right now.

Knock! Knock! Knock!

Couldn't they take a hint? She should have put a "Do Not Disturb" sign on the door. On the other hand, maybe it was Freya. Freya locked herself out of the room at least twice a week. Kimberly didn't really want to see Freya either, though. Freya had sung magnificently, and one of the music professors had already asked her to study with him privately.

Reluctantly, Kimberly rose from the bed and went to open the door.

"Can we come in?" Winnie asked glumly. She and KC stood in the hall. Winnie held a paper cup and a bag of Doritos. KC stood beside her, a bottle of mineral water dangling listlessly from her hand.

Kimberly hadn't thought anything could make her feel better, but the sight of her two depressed friends made her feel less alone.

"Wasn't the party any good?" Kimberly asked, ushering them into her room.

"I just wasn't in a party mood," Winnie said, taking a few quick strides across the room and sitting down on Kimberly's rag rug. She crossed her legs and settled the bag of Doritos between her knees. "All those couples dancing. It was just a painful reminder of the fact that I am *not* part of a couple."

"Tell me about it," KC said, sitting on Freya's bed. She unscrewed the cap on the mineral water and drank straight from the bottle. "How do you become a couple, anyway?" she asked, wiping away a few drops that had dribbled down her chin. "I mean, how do you determine which guys are going to stick around in a relationship and which ones are going to run away with no explanation?"

Kimberly lay back down on her bed and let her head sink into her soft down pillow. "I can't even answer questions about myself, let alone about that strange and foreign species: guys."

Winnie shoved another handful of Doritos into her mouth and chewed in silence. KC took another swig from her bottle. Kimberly shut her eyes.

"This is my kind of party," Kimberly murmured drowsily. "An anti-party party."

There was another knock on the door.

"More anti-partygoers," Winnie said, hopping up to answer the door.

"It's probably Freya," Kimberly said. "If she's too cheerful, we'll ask her to leave."

"I hope I'm not disturbing anything." It was Faith. Kimberly opened her eyes and sat up.

Faith stood in the doorway looking bleary-eyed. Her long, blond hair, which had looked so smooth earlier in the evening, now looked like it had been blowing around her head.

"Come in," Kimberly said. "That is, if you're still talking to me."

Faith sat down on Freya's bed next to KC. "Of course I'm still talking to you. Why wouldn't I?"

"I'm a fake and a failure," Kimberly said simply. "I should have warned you."

"Don't be so silly," Faith said. "Look on the bright side. Now that Liza had her chance to perform, maybe she'll be easier for me to live with. In a way, you did me a favor."

"So why aren't you downstairs at the cast party?" KC asked, offering Faith the mineral water. "Weren't you supposed to meet Sheldon there? He didn't stand you up, did he?"

Faith sighed and took a sip of water. "He was

there, right on time. After all, he did write it down on his schedule."

"And?" KC asked.

Faith shrugged. "I tried, KC. I really did. And he was every bit as gorgeous as you said. But we just didn't, you know, click."

"So, to sum it up," Kimberly said, "here we are, four dateless girls who are too depressed to even go to a party."

"Too bad Lauren's still at work," Faith said. "She's really in the dumps, literally, about her room. I'm sure she'd like to wallow in misery with us."

"But if we're all depressed," Winnie asked, "who's going to cheer us up?"

Kimberly, KC, and Faith all turned to look at Winnie resentfully.

"What?" Winnie asked. "Don't tell me you all prefer to sit here, feeling sorry for yourselves."

"It's an option," Kimberly said, laying back down on her bed.

"No!" Winnie said, hopping to her feet. "I haven't spent all those hours at the Crisis Hotline to let my own friends give in to depression. There must be something we can do to make ourselves feel better." She began pacing back and forth over the rag rug in her jingle bell boots.

"Can you work miracles?" KC asked. "If so, wave a magic wand and turn Peter back into a wonderful, caring guy?"

"While you're at it," Kimberly said, "could you erase my name from the memory of every single person who was at the show tonight?"

Faith raised her hand. "I've got a request, too. Could you turn Sheldon into my dream date and make Liza the perfect roommate?"

Winnie crossed her arms and looked at her friends in frustration. "I wish I could!" she said. "And while I was at it, I'd just materialize into Josh's room while he was alone. But none of you are looking at this constructively. You're only thinking about what we *can't* do. Let's think about what *can* be done."

"Okay, Winnie," Faith said. "How can we make the world a better place?"

"Let's not think about the whole world," Winnie said. "Let's just focus on one thing or one person."

"We could figure out a new career for me," Kimberly half-joked.

"We could have a support group for girls who've been dumped," KC said.

"Now we're cookin'," Winnie said. "Does anybody have any other ideas?"

Sixteen

t was ridiculous trying to work with the loud music coming from the lobby. The thumping bass line was traveling through the walls, making Peter's developing trays rattle. The solutions inside the trays rippled with tiny waves. But Peter was determined to keep busy. He'd been in his darkroom for almost an entire week, coming out only to eat and sleep and go to classes.

Peter knew his skin was white and pasty from so much time spent in the dark, and he hadn't shaved in three days, but he didn't care about his appearance. Even when he looked his best he wasn't goodlooking enough for KC, so what difference did it make whether he shaved or not?

A sudden silence hit Peter like a shockwave. The music had stopped. Was the Follies cast party really, finally over? Peter opened the door to his darkroom and saw groups of people digging out their jackets from a huge pile on the couch. Maybe now he could get some sleep. Peter ducked back inside, emptied his trays into the deep, industrial sink, and turned off his red light. Then he left the darkroom, locking the door behind him.

The dim light of the hallway seemed blindingly bright after so many hours in the dark. That's why he didn't recognize the tall, muscular jock until he was a few feet away. He'd only seen the guy once, but Peter would never forget his face for as long as he lived. It was KC's latest model-boyfriend, the one she'd been fondling last Saturday as they entered Coleridge Hall.

Peter looked around for KC. She had to be nearby. No doubt the two of them had come to the party together. So Peter was surprised she wasn't hanging off the guy like a barnacle. But he seemed to be alone.

As the guy paused in the hallway to put on his varsity jacket, Peter realized what he had to do. He didn't really blame this guy for stealing KC away from him. If KC was fickle and superficial, that was *her* fault, not this poor sucker's. No, Peter didn't blame him. He wanted to help him, to warn him against KC. It was the least he could do for a fellow male.

"Excuse me," Peter said, extending his hand. "I'm Peter Dvorsky and I'd like to have a word with you."

The guy took Peter's hand but looked confused. "Sheldon Copperstein," he said in a deep voice.

"Now you may think this weird, a complete stranger coming up to you, but I believe we have something in common."

"We do?" Sheldon asked. "Do you like stamps?"

Peter shook his head. "I guess I should have said *someone*. We have a mutual acquaintance. KC Angeletti."

Sheldon nodded. "Ah yes," he said. "An attractive girl."

"I see she's taken you in, too," Peter said. "But I wouldn't trust her if I were you."

"Trust?" Sheldon asked. "Trust was never a factor in our relationship."

"No kidding," Peter said. "I don't think she knows the meaning of the word."

"I wouldn't go that far," Sheldon said. "She seemed perfectly nice to me."

"You just haven't seen the other side of her yet," Peter said. "You'll see. She'll get you going, then leave you high and dry."

"I don't understand," Sheldon said, his dark eyebrows wrinkling. "Granted, I haven't known her very long, but she seemed dependable, and she was always on time for our appointments."

"Appointments?" Peter asked. That was an impersonal way to describe a date. But maybe that's why KC liked this guy. She was cold and impersonal, too. A human calculator with beautiful eyes.

"Our tutoring sessions," Sheldon explained. "What subject did you tutor her in?"

Now it was Peter's turn to be confused. "You tutored her? Is that how you started dating?"

"Dating?!" Sheldon said, surprised. "What are you talking about? I helped her write an essay for English. She did try to fix me up with her friend Faith, but I don't think it's going to work out. I'm not a chemistry major, but I can tell when the chemistry's missing."

This was too sudden for Peter. After all the agony he'd been through, he couldn't believe it had all been based on a misunderstanding. "But you did go up to KC's room," Peter said. "And she went to yours."

"They were convenient places to meet," Sheldon said.

"And all she did was try to fix you up with her friend?" Peter asked.

Sheldon shrugged. "Sorry to disappoint you," he said. "It sounds like you *want* to believe something happened."

"No, no," Peter said, backing up to the wall and leaning against it for support. "I just didn't want to believe I could have been so stupid."

"Look," Sheldon said, zipping up his jacket. "I hope you've cleared up your problem, whatever it is, but I've got to get some sleep. I've got an early meeting tomorrow morning of the Rare Stamp and Coin Collectors of America. I'm president of the U. of S. branch. See you." Sheldon gave a brief wave and headed toward the front door.

Peter slid down the wall and sat on the floor feeling like the world's biggest fool, with an even bigger broken heart. He'd let his insecurity do him in. KC hadn't dumped him. He'd just assumed she had because he couldn't believe such a beautiful, classy, intelligent girl could actually like a poor slob like himself. And by refusing to talk to her, he hadn't left himself open to learning the truth. Then he'd made it even worse by standing her up at her sorority dance. Now she would never talk to him again. He'd lost the most wonderful girl in the world, and it was all his fault.

"Sorry I'm late," Lauren said as she found Freya by the refreshment table in the Coleridge lobby. "I ended up working overtime at the Inn. One of the other maids was out sick, so we were short-handed."

"That's too bad," Freya said as she cut a bite of cake with her plastic fork. "You missed a great party and a great show. But I taped it for you."

"Thanks," Lauren said. "I can't wait to hear how you sounded."

Lauren searched the lobby for Faith and Kimberly, or any of her other ex-dormmates, but she didn't see many familiar faces and most people seemed to be leaving. "Where is everybody?" Lauren asked. "Didn't Faith or Kimberly come to their own cast party? And how about KC and Winnie? The only reason I came was to spend some time with them, and no one's here."

Freya shrugged. "I saw Faith just a little while ago. I thought I saw KC and Winnie, too. Kimberly never even showed up, though. I think she's feeling really bad that she couldn't go on tonight. She had an attack of stagefright."

Lauren's eyes widened in shock. "That's terrible! I should go talk to her, not that I could cheer her up much, in my current mood." Lauren checked her watch. "Well, since it's after midnight and everyone seems to be going home, I guess I'd better do the same before the streets get any more deserted."

Freya put a comforting hand on Lauren's shoulder. "Get home safely," she said.

Lauren slipped her green bomber jacket on and darted out the door. The air was chilly and damp as she marched quickly across the green. It felt like it was going to rain. Shivering, Lauren zipped up her jacket as she passed through the main gates of the campus.

If she walked quickly, she could be at her room in fifteen minutes. Not that she was in such a hurry to get home. The thought of spending another night in that tiny, dismal, rented *cell*— yes, that was the word—was not something she was looking forward to. Even though she'd finally saved up enough to buy a used, futon sleepsofa, she didn't have any other furniture. Her microwave, computer, and TV sat, side-by-side on the floor, covered by plastic in case there was another flood or cockroach attack. Her clothes still sat in boxes since she didn't have a dresser.

Lauren left the last decent block of stores and brownstones. Now it was time to really pick up speed as she passed a vacant lot, warehouses, and rundown tenements. While she hadn't had any trouble yet, Lauren couldn't let herself relax. The best way to avoid being assaulted was to be a moving target.

Sweating despite the chilly air, Lauren finally reached her block and her building, her key already in her hand. She stood by the rusty intercom as she let herself in through the battered door with its peeling gold numbers. An attack dog barked inside one of the ground floor apartments, as Lauren hurried up the narrow staircase.

Upon reaching the top floor, Lauren realized what the worst part was. It wasn't the bugs or the bad paint job or the leaky refrigerator. It was the loneliness. The mile between here and campus could have been a light-year. No one was going to come to see her all the way out here when they could stay on campus. The only living beings Lauren had to keep her company were the roaches.

Lauren sighed as she turned the key in her heavy-duty security lock. She'd just try to get to sleep as soon as she could and forget her grim surroundings.

When Lauren opened the door, the overhead light was on, as well as several lamps she didn't recognize. In fact, there was very little in the room that Lauren *did* recognize. Her futon was there, pushed against the far wall, but everything else was new. Half a dozen plants stood on milk crates beneath the windows. Fishnetting covered the wall above the futon. Posters for Broadway shows covered the other walls, and several more milk crates were stacked in the kitchen with bottles of soda, bags of chips, and pieces of cake. What had happened?

"Surprise!" shouted Winnie, KC, Faith, and Kimberly, as they tumbled out of the bathroom, with huge grins on their faces.

"Huh?" Lauren stood in the doorway, uncomprehending. "How did you guys get in here?"

"We bribed your landlady downstairs," Winnie said, smiling from ear to ear. "We showed her proof that we were your friends from school, and she let us in."

"But . . ." Lauren looked around the room again. It was no longer a grim hole, but a cheerful, stylish garret, perfect for a struggling artist like herself.

"Do you like it?" KC asked. "Winnie brought

the fishnetting, as I'm sure you've already figured out. Kimberly gave you the plants, Faith gave you the posters, and it was my bright idea to 'borrow' some of the refreshments from the Coleridge party. Oh yeah, and Courtney donated the lamps from the Tri Beta attic. We ran into her on our way across campus, and she insisted on helping. She's going to send over a couple of small tables, too, for your computer and TV."

Lauren felt tears starting to rise in her eyes. "I can't believe you all did this for me. I've never had friends like you in my entire life!"

Kimberly came forward to give Lauren a hug. "We feel the same way about you!"

As Faith, Winnie, and KC crowded around her, too, Lauren burst into tears. "Thank you," she said, trying to hug everyone at once. "Thank you all."

Seventeen

he next morning, still wearing her now-wrinkled black jumper and lacy blouse, Faith tramped through the damp grass of the dorm green. It had rained last night, so Lauren hadn't had any trouble talking her friends into sleeping over. Faith had been happy to keep Lauren company, and even happier to have an excuse not to spend the night in her room with Liza. It had been fun to huddle close together under the blankets, sheets, and comforter Lauren had.

This morning, they'd gone down to the deli to buy groceries and cooked a huge breakfast of blueberry pancakes, eggs, and fresh orange juice.

They'd eaten so much they all had stomach aches, but they'd had a terrific time. Of course, it was one more reminder that Lauren wasn't her roommate anymore, and Liza was.

Faith trudged up the stairs to her floor and wondered if Liza would be home. While Faith knew Liza would be in a great mood since her brilliant success, Faith still wasn't looking forward to seeing her. Liza would probably make her listen to fifteen minutes of Why-you-should-have-cast-me-in-the-first-place. And the worst part was, maybe Liza would be right.

Faith opened the door and smelled something fragrant and sweet. Was this Liza's new perfume? Liza wasn't there, but a huge bouquet of exotic flowers was standing on Faith's desk.

The smell grew more intense as Faith reached for the little white envelope stuck among the blossoms. She opened it and pulled out a card which said:

Faith,
Thank you so much! When I write my autobiography, I'm going to say you gave me my first break!
Love,
Liza

So Liza had been a good sport! Maybe they'd end up being friends, after all. Faith buried her face in the blossoms, and her nose began to tickle. The smell was overwhelming. Unbearable even. *Hachoo! Hachoo!* Faith sneezed. *Hachoo!*

"Mmmmm," Winnie inhaled deeply. "I love the smell after it rains. It's like the world is getting a brand new start." She and KC cut across the damp green under the sunny sky. After walking back to campus with Faith, they'd split off to head to their dorms.

"For a girl who didn't sleep more than two hours last night, you're in a cheerful mood," KC observed. "Was it the pancakes?"

"Partly," Winnie said. "But I just feel like I'm going to get a brand new start, too. Maybe when I walk through the door of Forest Hall, Josh will be waiting for me again, and this time we'll finally work things out. He wants to and I want to, and he handed in his research paper. All the obstacles are gone."

"It will work out," KC said with a sad smile. She only wished her relationship with Peter had half as much hope, or any hope at all. But it was over, and there was no chance of bringing it back to life.

Even before the girls came up over a hill and

saw Forest Hall, Winnie was already quickening her pace. Her eyes were shining as she looked at her sterile, motel-like dorm, like it was the most beautiful place on earth. "I'll talk to you soon," Winnie said, giving KC a quick peck on the cheek. Then she dashed down the hill.

With a sigh, KC walked the rest of the way alone. She trudged up the stairs of Langston House, walked across the front porch and through the old oak door. She looked around nervously, wondering whether anyone would notice she was wearing the same clothes as the night before. She knew how that would look to suspicious minds. Little would they know that she'd had a great guy in her life, but that now he was gone. KC still hadn't figured out why Peter had turned on her suddenly. She knew she hadn't done anything wrong. There had to be something wrong with *him*. But what? And when would she be able to stop thinking about him all the time, and stop feeling so much pain?

When KC reached the top of the stairs, she saw a lump of blue denim on the floor at the end of the hall. It looked like it was in front of her room. Had someone left their laundry outside her door?

As KC got closer, she saw it wasn't laundry. It was a person in blue jeans and a blue jeans jacket, lying curled up in a ball. KC gasped when she realized who it was.

"Peter!" she said, half to herself, half-aloud.

Peter mumbled something and rolled over onto his back, still sleeping. KC gazed down at him tenderly. Was he having a bad dream? KC wanted to wrap him in her arms and tell him that everything would be okay.

Peter's eyelids started to flutter. Then he opened his eyes. As soon as he saw her, a smile lit up his face and KC found herself smiling, too. Then she remembered that Peter had stood her up, given her the silent treatment, and now he dared to show up like a package on her doorstep? KC scowled.

Peter ran his hands through his already messy, light brown hair. Then he stiffly rose to his feet. "I suppose you're wondering why I'm sleeping in your hallway," he said, looking down at his sneakers.

"Actually, Peter," KC said coolly, "I couldn't care less why you do anything. I'm surprised the janitor hasn't swept you away with the rest of the trash."

Peter pressed his lips together and shoved his hands into the pockets of his denim jacket. "Okay," he said. "I understand completely why you feel that way, and I don't blame you a bit. I also understand why you were gone all night. You've already found another boyfriend. But that's none of my business."

"How do you know I was gone all night?" KC asked.

Peter gestured at the floor by KC's door. "I slept here," he said.

"All night?" KC asked.

"Well, no, not exactly," Peter said. "The floor advisor kicked me out at midnight, so I slept on the grass outside your dorm. I came back in around eight o'clock this morning. I guess I fell asleep again."

KC couldn't bear the thought of how cold and uncomfortable Peter must have been all night. But she wasn't about to let him know that. "That was stupid," she said. "What were you trying to do—catch pneumonia?"

"I wanted to talk to you," Peter said. "Not that I expect you to listen to me. But I wanted to explain why I never showed up at your sorority dance so that even if things are over between us, at least you'll know I wasn't a complete jerk."

"Too late," KC said. "I've already reached that conclusion. Now, if you don't mind, would you please stop blocking my doorway? I'd like to go inside." KC tried to get around Peter, but he blocked her with his body. For several seconds, they stared each other down. KC tried to keep her expression fierce, but she could feel herself softening inside.

"Why didn't you just tell me in the dining commons when I tried to talk to you?" KC demanded. "Wouldn't that have been a whole lot more convenient than sleeping in my hall?"

"I didn't know then what I know now," Peter said. "You see, I thought you'd dumped me for that guy Sheldon. A girl on your floor told me she saw you together, and then I saw the two of you in my dorm, and it looked like you were all lovey-dovey, and I assumed the worst. Now I realize the problem wasn't you, or anything you did. It was *me*. I'm so insecure I just figured you'd throw me over for the next good-looking guy who came along. I guess I should have trusted you more."

"More?" KC demanded. "I don't think you trusted me at all."

"No," Peter admitted, looking down at his sneakers again. "And now I've got to suffer for it. I don't deserve you, and maybe what this proves is that you really are too good for me."

KC let her eyes rest on Peter's fine, silky hair. They traveled down his faded jacket, rumpled jeans, and his scuffling, sneakered feet. "So you think I'm too good for you?" she asked in a stern voice.

Peter looked up again with such a mixture of pain, love, and despair that KC thought she was going to cry. "I know you are," he said.

"Do you want to know what I think?" KC asked.

Peter nodded, his brown eyes anxious.

"This is what I think," KC said, stepping forward and wrapping her arms around Peter. His denim jacket was still a little damp, so KC pulled it down off his shoulders and let it drop to the floor. Then she slid her fingers into the back pockets of his jeans, and standing on tiptoe, she closed her eyes, and found his lips with her own.

Here's a sneak preview of Freshman Fling, the eleventh book in the dramatic story of FRESHMAN DORM.

"**S**o where are you?" Kimberly drummed her fingers on one of the tables in the empty physics lab.

She looked at the stool where her lab partner, Derek Weldon, should be sitting. "Whoever you are—wherever you are—Derek Weldon, you'd better get your sorry self into this room in the next five minutes or I'm leaving."

Suddenly the door banged open and a tall mass of energy draped in black pleated pants and a blue shirt strode forward. Kimberly stared. His skin was what her grandmother called "coffee and two creams." And his brown eyes, even behind their wire-rimmed glasses, were big enough to fall into.

"You're late," was all she could think to say.

Derek stopped, staring at her. He shrugged his shoulders and sauntered to the table. "It's not my fault I need twenty-eight hours in the day to do everything I want to do." He plunked his book-bag down on the table.

"Well," said Kimberly, trying to ignore the strange flutter in her stomach, "it certainly isn't my fault, either. You're not the only one around here with things to do."

"I'll match my day against yours any time," he said, sliding onto a stool. "I'm very involved in *This Week at the U.*"

Kimberly folded her arms tight across her chest, trying to keep her anger down. "Well," she said, "since your time is so *very* precious, perhaps we should get started."

"You know, it wouldn't kill you to be just a little sympathetic."

"About what? You don't come to class. You don't call me when you know perfectly well Prof. Jobst said you were supposed to. You keep me waiting fifteen minutes in this lab until you're good and ready to show up, and—"

"Hey, calm down. This is only one experiment. It's no big deal."

"And you're making me late for my rehearsal," Kimberly said, finishing the sentence he'd interrupted. "Of course, my dance performance isn't *nearly* as important as anything going on in your life. Except," she said slapping her hand on the counter, and making Derek jump, "it's something I've been training for my whole life. Except," she slapped the counter again, "I need all the time I can get to work on it. So don't you go telling me to be calm, Mr. I-Have-So-Much-To-Do. And don't you be deciding what is or is not a big deal in my life."

Derek's jaw moved back and forth as he clenched his teeth. "Then maybe we'd better get started," he said, trying to control his anger.

"Good." Kimberly opened a book. "I brought some library books on—"

"Here." He reached into his pocket and pulled out two large balloons. "Blow one up."

"You are a crazy person," said Kimberly.

"That's what they say about all great scientists." His smile caught her off guard and she smiled back before remembering how angry she was at him. "Now, this experiment is supposed to be about action-reaction, right?"

"Right."

"Something cannot be pushed, unless something else is pushing."

"That's what the law says."

"And something can't push unless there is something *to* push. Right?"

Kimberly nodded. He might be late and he might be arrogant, but Derek was also bright.

"Okay. We have a balloon. That's one thing. Then we have the air inside. That's another thing. Now, how do we show one pushing against the other and the other pushing back?" He let the balloon go and it zoomed around the room, diving and climbing, making crazy circles and waves, until it ran out of air and dropped to the floor.

"The air pushing against the balloon, the balloon pushing against the air inside, propels the balloon forward," Derek went on. "Action-reaction." He climbed down from the table. "Well? What do you think?"

Kimberly was speechless. She couldn't believe she'd spent so many hours at the library, weeding through advanced physics books, only to end up with an experiment that any second grader could do. "That's your entire experiment?"

"I have enough balloons for everyone in class," Derek answered. "This experiment fulfills Prof. Jobst's requirements and, I think, it'll be fun. So I guess now we're set." He smiled, grabbed his things, and walked out of the room, leaving a stunned Kimberly to wonder whether she should laugh or cry or scream. *Maybe,* she thought, *I should do all three.*